"This is just a crop moon," the old fella said. "Don't think you'll find what you—"

In a tight voice, Mal told the man, in Chinese, to shut up and make them wealthy.

Seeing the wisdom of Mal's words—or at least the wisdom of their big guns—the old fella entered a code into the keypad next to the vault. Mal then opened it right up.

Jayne had been itching to shoot someone all day, and that itch just got a lot harder not to scratch. The vault wasn't exactly empty, but it was as close as made no never mind. Maybe three bills, some scattered coin. What was in that vault would barely cover the fuel for the mule's trip to and from *Serenity*.

Zoë looked at Mal. "At last," she said dryly, "we can retire and give up this life of crime."

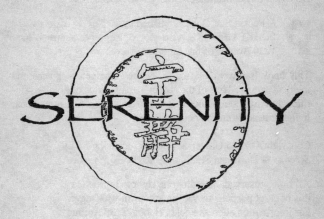

SERENITY

A Novel by Keith R.A. DeCandido

Based on the motion picture screenplay
by Joss Whedon

POCKET STAR BOOKS
New York London Toronto Sydney

An *Original* Publication of POCKET BOOKS

A Pocket Star Book published by
POCKET BOOKS, a division of Simon & Schuster, Inc.
1230 Avenue of the Americas, New York, NY 10020

This book is a work of fiction. Names, characters, places and incidents are products of the author's imagination or are used fictitiously. Any resemblance to actual events or locales or persons, living or dead, is entirely coincidental.

ISBN-13: 978-1-4165-0755-0
ISBN-10:   1-4165-0755-8

First Pocket Books paperback edition September 2005

10 9 8 7 6 5 4 3 2 1

POCKET STAR BOOKS and colophon are registered trademarks of Simon & Schuster, Inc.

Manufactured in the United States of America

For information regarding special discounts for bulk purchases, please contact Simon & Schuster Special Sales at 1-800-456-6798 or business@simonandschuster.com.

For Nathan, Gina, Alan, Jewel, Morena, Adam, Sean,
Summer, and Ron . . .

Oh yeah, and that Joss fella, too . . .

SERENITY

First Prelude:

THE WAR

SERENITY VALLEY, HERA

Sergeant Malcolm Reynolds's life had reduced itself to the critical imperative of running.

He pumped his legs as fast as he could through the uneven ground of Serenity Valley, his boots slamming down onto the rocks and dirt. With a determination born of faith and righteousness, he ignored the aching muscles, the fingers that desperately wanted to relinquish their grip on his weapon, and the bodies of so many of his fellow soldiers as he dashed back to base camp. Not to mention the mortar fire lighting up the night sky all around him.

"Base camp" was probably a more highfalutin name than the pile of sandbags in the dirt deserved, but that was what they had. The tattered remains of the Independent defense was headquartered there.

For five weeks, they had held the valley. Serenity Valley was the key to Hera, and Hera was the key to the war. Whoever controlled this particular ball of rock would be in position to do considerable damage to the other side.

Doing damage was a notion Mal Reynolds could surely get behind.

He stumbled up the incline that led to base camp, throwing his arms down at the last minute to cushion the impact as his body hit the ground. *That,* he thought, *could've been ugly. Might've split my lip or something.*

It was a weak joke, but such were powerful funny when you were watching Alliance aircraft mow down platoon after platoon after platoon.

To some extent, Mal was flattered by the attention. The Alliance calling in air support meant that they took the Browncoats' defense of Serenity Valley seriously—something they probably commenced to doing after a month had passed without the Alliance taking Serenity in twenty-four hours like they planned.

So they sent in more troops. And more air support.

As Mal watched, an Alliance skiff took down dozens of his people, plowing through bodies like knives.

Stumbling into base camp, he wondered where the hell their own air support was. The Alliance had been too clever by half, and made sure to target officers instead of grunts. Mal wasn't all sure, but it seemed fair to certain that he was the highest-ranking Browncoat left in this gorram valley.

And still we're holding it. He smiled. These Alliance folk were getting a hard lesson in the power of positive thinking—in this case, the people were positive they didn't need some government completely taking over their lives. The Alliance was welcome to the central planets, but keep your grubby mitts off our outer worlds, thank you *so* much. *Once our air support shows up, then you'll really see what we can do.* Until then, though, that Alliance skiff out there was not going to let up until all the Browncoats were dead.

He went straight for the corporal whose name he could not remember, but who he called "Grin" on account of how he never once smiled. Grin was from Sergeant DeLorenzo's platoon, until Sergeant DeLorenzo—and three-quarters of his platoon—were wiped out by the first Alliance airplane to show up.

At Mal's questioning glance, Grin said, "Sergeant, Command says they're holding until they can assess our status."

Mal's jaw fell open. "Our status is, we need some gorram air support. Now get back online, tell 'em to get in here!" *What is it about Command that they must insist on having their heads firmly implanted in their rectums?*

Even as Mal spoke, Zoë Alleyne leapt in from above. "That skiff is shredding us, sir."

Zoë had been with Mal in the 57th from the beginning of the war, and it hadn't taken long for him to count on her as his right hand. Mal knew he was a decent soldier, all things considered, but Zoë was brilliant. There were times when Mal was convinced that, had Zoë been on the Alliance's side, this war would be over, and the Browncoats would be done for. And had there been more like Zoë, he suspected that a lot more of his people would be alive. As it was, only he, Zoë, Bendis, and McAvoy were left of the original 57th, though he had inherited plenty of others, including the entire company under Lieutenant

Baker's command, owing to Lieutenant Baker lying dead with several dozen bullets in his chest not three meters from where Mal was crouched down right present.

Grin was fixing Mal with his usual serious expression. "They won't move without a lieutenant's authorization code, sir."

Firmly implanted in their gorram rectums. Mal ran over to Baker's corpse, muttered a quick prayer and apology—Ben Baker wasn't a bad sort for an officer—and ripped the ID patch off the lieutenant's uniform arm. On the underside was etched the man's code.

Handing Grin the patch, Mal said, "Here—here's your code. You're Lieutenant Baker, congratulations on your promotion, now get me some *air support!*"

Mal then gathered Zoë, McAvoy, Johannsen, Tedesco, and Bendis to his side. Mal had put McAvoy in charge of one of the squads, which was made up entirely of the remnants of fifteen other squads. Since the air support was taking its good sweet time, they needed themselves a Plan B. Luckily, he'd seen the makings of that plan down the hill a ways, since the Alliance had been right neighborly enough to not blow up the GAG when they wiped out the 32nd.

To Johannsen and Tedesco: "Pull back just far enough to wedge 'em in here." To McAvoy: "Get your squad to high ground, start pickin' 'em off."

McAvoy nodded, but Zoë looked pissed. "High ground is death with that skiff in the air," she said.

"That's *our* job." He gave her a cheeky grin. "Thanks

6

for volunteering." Then he looked at the youngest member of the squad. "Bendis, give us some cover fire—we're goin' duck hunting."

Suddenly the entire base camp rattled and shook as mortar fire landed close enough to send everyone sprawling. Without even thinking, Mal threw his hands over his face to protect his eyes from the dust and dirt and shrapnel.

When he removed his arms, Johannsen lay dead in front of him. Bendis was staring at the corpse, eyes wide, lips quivering, his hands gripping his rifle so hard his knuckles were even whiter than his face.

Mal grabbed his shoulder. "You just *focus!*" He looked in turn at each of the others. Tedesco didn't look so hot, either, and McAvoy was biting down on his lower lip so hard he was drawing blood. They'd come too far to start giving up now. "The Alliance said they were just gonna waltz through Serenity Valley, and we choked them with those words. We have done the impossible and that makes us mighty." He smiled, hoping to give them the confidence he felt, because Mal knew that soon this battle would be over and they would be the victors. "Just a little while longer and our angels will be soarin' overhead raining fire on those arrogant cusses, so you hold."

He looked Bendis right in the eye. "You *hold!*"

After a moment, he said, "Go!" McAvoy, Bendis, Tedesco, Zoë, and the others all moved to ready their weapons.

As she reloaded her weapon, Zoë shot Mal a look. Mal had come to know—and appreciate—that as

Zoë's I-know-you-want-us-to-feel-better-but-are-you-just-bullshitting-us? expression. "You really think we can bring her down, sir?"

Mal grinned. "You even need to ask?"

His weapon already primed, Mal took a moment to pull the crucifix out from under his shirt. Kissing it, he whispered a quick "Our Father." Mal wasn't arrogant enough to think of the Independence cause to be the same as the way Christ defied the Romans, but he was also wise enough to see the similarities. The Alliance swallowed planets with technology and rule of law and conformity. Mal had nothing against technology, and rule of law certainly had its place in the 'verse, but conformity was not a concept he could get behind, any more than Christ could.

Prayer completed, Mal got to his feet. "Ready?"

"Always." Zoë was, of course, right behind him. God and Zoë were the only two things in the 'verse Mal Reynolds had counted on, and neither one of them had let him down yet.

The same could not be said for Bendis, who was not right behind Zoë. In fact, he hadn't moved a muscle since Mal told him to hold.

"Bendis!" Zoë bellowed in a voice that could command the stars to change alignment.

But Bendis still didn't move, even after two more yells from Zoë.

McAvoy had already moved off, and his people would be in position in five minutes. They couldn't afford to wait—or to babysit Bendis. Mal nodded to Zoë, who hauled herself and her weapon above the sandbags and started laying down Bendis's cover fire.

Mal ran out from behind the bags and started his run toward the GAG.

Ground-air guns were a handy weapon to have when faced with air strikes by Alliance skiffs. The Alliance, however, knew that, and so made sure that the soldiers assigned to the only GAG the Browncoats had in Serenity Valley were their primary target. Mal's goal was to get to it and take that gorram skiff down before it picked off the entire damn company.

When he got to the rock-line—Zoë, naturally, right behind him—he peered down to make sure that what he saw half an hour earlier still held true. Sure enough, there was only one Alliance soldier guarding the GAG. Mal wondered if it was overconfidence, or if it was just that their troops were spread too thin. Then Mal decided he didn't rightly care all that much, long as it remained so.

Pausing to take aim at the soldier—who at least had the good sense to be under some cover—Mal fired.

The Alliance soldier lay dead moments later.

Mal recollected something a shepherd had said to him round a year or so back: The commandment was not "You will not kill," as it was often mistranslated. It was, in fact, "You will not commit murder."

As far as Mal was concerned, though he'd killed many a person since this war commenced, he'd yet to murder a single living soul.

He ran down to the GAG, Zoë staying behind to watch his back. Settling into the shoulder harness, he activated the weapon—thanking the good Lord that the Alliance hadn't actually sabotaged the thing—and swiveled it up and around toward the skiff that had been making their lives a ruttin' hell for the past hour.

The compglass lit up with targeting information. Mal let the computer do its job, setting the GAG's sights on the skiff and staying with it once the target was acquired.

Then, when a low beep, barely audible over the shell fire all around him, told him that the skiff was in range, he fired.

Two barrels loaded with two-hundred-caliber ammunition fired at full strength into the skiff at Mal's command, tearing through that flying deathtrap as easily as the skiff's own bullets went through Mal's people.

Stepping out of the GAG, Mal whooped and cheered as the skiff went hurtling down—

—right toward him on the ground.

Tzao-gao!

Turning, Mal ran as fast as he could, pumping his tired, aching legs as hard as he could. 'Cause it would be right embarrassing to go to all that trouble to shoot down the skiff and then get oneself crushed by its flaming, descending hulk. That sort of thing could ruin a man's day.

"Zoë!" he cried as he ran toward her. She whirled around to see a crazed sergeant barreling right for her, a fiery skiff heading toward the ground at a great rate right behind him.

Even as Mal grabbed her, she herself leapt to the ground, hoping to avoid the wreck.

Mal felt the heat of the explosion on his back, and for a moment, he feared his coat would catch fire.

Then the explosion started to die down. Mal rolled over on his back and started laughing.

Zoë gave him her you're-ruttin'-insane-sir look.

They ran back to base camp. Mal couldn't stop laughing. *We are going to take this valley, we are going to take this rock, and we are going to win this thing!*

As they ran back behind the sandbags, Mal saw Bendis, who had yet to budge from his spot. Zoë looked like she was going to spit at him. "Nice cover fire!"

Mal, however, couldn't bring himself to be angry. "Did you *see* that?" He ran over to the radio. "Grin, what's our status on—?"

Then he saw that Grin was lying down on the job. Not really his fault, mind, seeing as he had a bullet hole where his left temple used to be, Baker's patch still clutched in his hand.

Looking away, Mal called for Zoë and pointed at the radio. She nodded and ran over to Grin's corpse, taking the headpiece out of his right ear.

Mal instead went over to Bendis, who looked like he had soiled himself a dozen times over. "Hey, listen to me, Bendis." Gritting his teeth, he yelled, "Look at me!" Bendis finally looked up at him. Mal saw considerable fear in the boy's eyes. "Listen—we're holding this valley no matter what."

For the first time in what seemed like days, Bendis spoke, in a dull monotone. "We're gonna die."

11

"We're *not* gonna die. We can't die, Bendis, and you know why? Because we are so very pretty." He grinned. "We are just too pretty for God to let us die. Huh?" He grabbed Bendis's chin. *"Look* at that chiseled jaw. Huh? C'mon."

The beginnings of the possibility of a smile started to consider appearing on Bendis's face. But before Mal could commence to trying to cheer the boy up further, the sound he'd been waiting all night for finally made itself heard through the weapons fire.

Air support.

He couldn't tell if it was one big ship or a whole passel of little ones, and he didn't rightly care. Looking up and grinning even wider, he said to Bendis, "Well, if you won't listen to me, listen to that." He looked at Bendis. "Those are our angels, come to send the Alliance to the hot place." Turning back toward the radio, he said, "Zoë, tell the 82nd—"

"They're not coming."

At first Mal assumed he heard wrong. *Of course the 82nd's coming, I can hear them, they're—*

Then he heard it. The tone in Zoë's voice. He recognized it on account of Zoë not normally having much by way of a tone. On anyone else, it would've just sounded like a monotone, but there were nuances to Zoë's speaking patterns that one learned to suss out if one got to spending enough time with her.

And what Mal heard now was despair as deep as what he saw in Bendis's eyes.

"Command says it's too hot," Zoë said. "They're pulling out. We're to lay down arms."

Lay down arms?

No. Mal refused to believe it. They were *winning,* gorramit, they were beating back the Alliance, and God was on their side, and they were *winning!*

Besides, he *heard* the angels. "But what's—?"

Then he realized.

Even though he knew he couldn't bear to see it, he forced himself to stand up and look over the sandbags. Bendis stood up next to him.

It wasn't the 82nd he heard, though he had, in fact, heard angels. They were the seven angels who heralded the end of the world.

"The first angel sounded his trumpet, and there came hail and fire mixed with blood, and it was hurled down upon the earth. A third of the earth was burned up, a third of the trees were burned up, and all the green grass was burned up."

For all the weeks they'd been holding Serenity Valley, the sounds of battle had become so much white noise to Mal. Now, though, it was like all his senses were more acute than ever.

He smelled the acrid ozone of the bullets flying through the air, including the one that struck Bendis in the chest, killing him instantly as he stood next to Mal.

He felt the ground shake as the Alliance vessels' thrusters slammed against the ground to permit them a soft landing.

He tasted the bitter adrenaline combined with bile at the realization of what was happening.

He heard Zoë say that the Independents were asking the Alliance for a parley to discuss terms of surrender.

And he saw hail and fire being hurled down upon the earth, and mixing with the blood of the people Mal Reynolds had called comrades.

— —

Zoë had thought she had seen the worst possible ways to die.

She believed that the Alliance didn't have the right to control all the known worlds. The Alliance, naturally, had something to say about that, so there was a war. Zoë had fought, going where they told her to, shooting what they told her to shoot. That was what she did. Zoë had no illusions—she was a follower. She was particular about who she chose *to* follow, mind, but she knew her limitations. Unlike, say, Malcolm Reynolds, she had no leadership skills.

But she had a fair portion of fighting skills, and she was sure to put them all to good use against the Alliance.

She thought she had seen all the worst ways to die during the war.

That was before the fighting stopped.

It had been two weeks. A fortnight since Command said Serenity Valley was "too hot" after they'd held it for so long. Fourteen days since they were told to lay down arms.

Two weeks since they'd been left there to wait until the armistice was signed.

Two weeks to watch people die.

There were no proper medical facilities on this part of Hera, and they had no way to get to the places that did. No ships flew overhead while they waited, no chatter came over the radio.

So people died. They died of wounds that got infected. They died of colds that they might have shaken off in a day if they weren't exposed and exhausted and bleeding. They died when they fought over what little food remained. They died when they decided eating their pistols was a better end than waiting in Serenity Valley for hope that would not show itself.

For Zoë's part, she dealt with it by shutting off her feelings. It was the only way to surround yourself with suffering—and also the only way to inflict it on other people. It didn't get to her because she refused to let it.

Throughout it all, Sergeant Mal Reynolds kept the troops going as best he could. Anyone else in charge, Zoë was sure they'd all be dead. But he managed to keep everyone going, with jokes, with inspiration, with anything he could throw at them.

Except, she noticed after the third day, for hope. The hope that he had instilled in the troops from day one was gone. Had Zoë not been so concerned with whether or not she'd starve to death, she might have mentioned it. As it was, she was content to let him be.

On the fifteenth day, Kiri said, "I can hear something. Does anybody hear that?"

Zoë refrained from answering that the only things

she could hear were, alternately, her stomach grumbling or Tedesco's labored breathing as he tried to gasp air with a chest that was riddled with bullet holes.

Sergeant Reynolds called out, "Corporal! Zoë! Signal flares!"

Struggling to rise, Zoë asked, "Whose colors?" As she forced her limbs to crawl through the fatigue, the injury, the agony, she noticed that Tedesco wasn't breathing at all. That in fact he'd been dead for two days since being shot in the face. *So why did I think I was hearing his breathing?*

Kiri said, "It's a rescue ship, sir! They came! They came. . . ." Kiri sounded like she couldn't believe it.

Zoë couldn't believe that no one answered her question. "Whose *colors* are they flying?" She also couldn't get up. Her legs, on which she hadn't called often these past two days, had taken to that state of affairs and simply refused to function.

And then, there was the sergeant, offering her a helping hand. There were few things in the 'verse Zoë could count on. Malcolm Reynolds was one of them.

"It don't matter none," he said in a quiet voice. "One side or the other, it makes no difference."

Zoë couldn't believe her ears. If it didn't make a difference, what had they been fighting for?

Sergeant Reynolds turned to Kiri and Bourke, who was standing next to him. "Both of you, pass the word. See who's still with us." Then he bellowed,

"Look alive, people! We got medships en route! We need to prepare for extraction!"

It took all Zoë's willpower to keep from bursting out laughing. "Extraction," indeed. Well, actually, it took no willpower, as she could barely stand up, but still, the notion was crazy. They weren't being "extracted." You were extracted when you were being removed from an op that was over. This—this was just vultures picking over the bones to see if there was any good meat left.

She rooted through a supply bag for the flare, then looked up at the sky. The ships were starting to come into view now, but they were still pretty much just specks against the clouds. Then she handed the sergeant the flare and asked the question she was afraid to ask, yet had to: "Are those really medships? Are we really getting out?"

He took the flare and said, "We are."

For the first time in two weeks, Zoë allowed herself to feel something: relief. "Thank God." She let out a long breath, and even thought about the possibility of smiling a little.

Sergeant Reynolds looked at her with as disgusted an expression as she'd ever seen on his face. "God?" He lit the flare. "Whose colors *he* flyin'?"

Zoë shot him a look. *He really has lost it.*

Then she remembered the old saying about how there were no atheists in foxholes. By the same token, there weren't very many worshippers in charnel houses, and that's what Serenity Valley was. The dead outnumbered the living by at least ten to one. Zoë had gotten so used to the odor of death that she suspected that the inside of the medship—and it was a medship, she could see that now as it came closer—would smell peculiar.

Either way, the war was finally over. And they lost.

Second Prelude:
THE ACADEMY

OSIRIS

Dr. Simon Tam pounced on the letter from his sister like a hungry man attacking a meal.

At least, Simon assumed it was the same. Having grown up in one of the wealthier families in the Alliance, and having even at his young age carved out an impressive career as a physician, he had never known hunger. He knew of the concept only from textbooks he'd read.

The latest letter started with the words, "I hope all is well with you, my favorite brother." Skipping to the end, he saw that the last sentence read, "My next book to read is *Triumph of the Terraformers,* by Wu Baifang."

If the code—which had taken him several missives to figure out—held true, the key to the code would be in Wu's book, which was on River's bookshelf. River had always had a fondness for codex books, and the Tams were rich enough to indulge that. Most publishers were willing to print a leather-bound copy of a book for the right price.

Please don't let Mother and Father have given it away to the library. . . . Wu's book was a particularly lurid treatise on the terraforming of the system that was the first step in colonizing after Earth-That-Was was used up. Nobody took it particularly seriously as history. River only liked it because she enjoyed Wu's use of language.

Minutes later, he found it on her shelf—right next to Detlev Woczynski's novel *Moonward Ho!*—and minutes after that, he confirmed that this letter, like every other one she'd sent in the past two months, was in the code.

Simon spent the next hour pacing in his room, waiting for his parents to come home from whatever function they were attending. Simon hadn't been able to go, as his shift ended two hours into the event. Besides, Simon hadn't been much in the mood for partying lately.

Lately—more like the last nine months. That was how long it had been since River went off to the prosaically named Alliance Academy. None of the Tams had ever heard of it, but their program was spectacular. Father had checked around, and discovered that the government-sponsored school came with the highest recommendations.

Ultimately, though, it was River's enthusiasm for the program that sold them. At the tender age of fourteen, she was already at a level that exceeded that of most universities. Every other school she looked at bored her to tears, as it was the equivalent of sending the chief resident Simon worked for in Capital City Hospital to an undergraduate biology class.

The academy was the only program that got her

excited. That alone was reason enough for her to go.

After the first few letters, nothing had come from the academy. Simon hadn't been concerned at first—he was kept busy enough at the hospital—but after a while, he started to worry.

Then the letters started coming regularly. They were utter nonsense—at first.

Until he cracked the code.

When his parents came home, the first thing he said was, "We got another letter today. River is in trouble."

Father rolled his eyes. "We're fine, son, thanks for asking, and we had a wonderful time. The Crosettis asked after you. You know, their daughter's always had her eye on you, and—"

"I don't *care* about the Crosettis, I care about my sister." He walked back to the breakfront to retrieve the letters.

Sighing, Mother said, "Your sister is *fine,* Simon."

"She's *not* fine. Didn't you look at the letters? *Look* at the letters!"

Rolling his eyes a second time, Father took the most recent batch of letters from Simon's hand. His eyes, having finished rolling, now looked down at River's perfect handwriting. "I'm looking at letters."

"These phrases," Simon said impatiently, "they don't sound *anything* like her. She called me her 'favorite' brother—which isn't all that much of a compliment when you consider that I'm her *only* brother." He grabbed another letter and practically shoved it in Mother's face. "Some of these words—they're misspelled."

Both parents looked at him blankly.

Speaking slowly, Simon said, "She started correcting *my* spelling when she was *three*. She's trying to tell us something. I think there's a code."

Father laughed. Mother's jaw fell open. "A *code?*"

Saying it out loud made it sound much sillier than it had in Simon's head. "Yes."

Shaking his head, Father said, "I always thought it was River who was lost without her big brother, but now I'm starting to wonder if it wasn't the other way around."

Simon refused to give up. "Did you have a good time at the d'Arbanvilles' ball this year?"

Predictably, both of them provided another blank look. This one, though, made a bit more sense.

Holding up last week's letter, Simon said, "River thought it was duller than last year. But since we don't know anybody named d'Arbanville, I'm having trouble judging. Did you even *read* these?"

Indignantly, Father said, "Of course I did."

"It's one of her silly games." Mother spoke as if it was the only possible explanation. "You two are always playing."

Simon was starting to wonder if Mother and Father had ever paid any attention to either of them. Mother's rationalization made a certain sense—when River and Simon were preteens. But Simon was an adult now, and though still a teenager, River was a lot more mature than most adults Simon knew.

The siblings had been inseparable for as long as Simon could remember, and a horrible truth was dawning on him as he listened to his parents so completely misunderstand what he was saying: River and Simon spent so much time together because they didn't have anyone else. They shared a house with these two people who gave them birth, but they shared a life only with each other.

Still, he persevered. "She is trying to tell us something that someone doesn't want her to say. Every letter has ended with her mentioning a book she is reading next—each time it's been a book on her shelf."

"Simon—"

Interrupting Father, he said, "Please, let me finish. The first word of each letter is always one, two, or three letters long—that indicates whether it should be the first, second, or third letter of each word that I pay attention to for the code. That letter corresponds to a number from one to twenty-six, and the first letter on that particular page is the next letter in the message she's sending. Every letter—*every* single letter—has the same message: 'They're hurting us. Get me out.'"

Now Mother looked concerned. She stepped forward and put what she probably thought was a comforting hand on Simon's arm. "Simon, this is paranoid. This is stress. If they heard you talking like this at the hospital, it could affect your entire future."

Simon was aghast. "Who *cares* about my future?"

"You should." Father had barely been taking the proceedings seriously, but now his tone grew much more grave.

"You are a surgeon in one of the best hospitals in

Capital City, on your way to a major position, possibly even the Medical Elect." Mother spoke as if this was some kind of revelation. "You're going to throw all that away? Everything you've worked for your whole life?"

Father, still serious, but kinder this time, added, "Being a doctor means more to you than just a position—I know that." He put a hand on Simon's shoulder, which felt as cold and lifeless as Mother's similar gesture moments ago.

"In a few months' time," Mother said, "you'll turn around, and there she'll be. Nothing is going to keep you two apart for long."

That was the first thing Mother said in the entire conversation that Simon actually believed.

—

The few months went by, with the letters still coming, the code still intact, and Mother and Father just as oblivious. They didn't care about River, or about Simon, they just cared about their position. River was at a government-sponsored academy, Simon was a rising star in the medical community. They weren't children so much as they were something to talk about at dinner parties—status symbols.

As the next two years went by, Simon tried to get in to see River. Nothing worked. He had even gone to a Blackout Zone to talk to someone who might help him out, but all that did was get him arrested and yelled at by Father.

The arrest didn't even slow Simon down.

The letters became increasingly more incoherent. The code was no longer in effect, but the tone of the letters—and the inconsistency of what used to be picture-perfect handwriting—led Simon to think that she wasn't capable of holding the code in her head.

One day, he went in to see a patient named Guillermo Garcia, who was complaining of gastric distress. That wasn't Simon's area of expertise, and he normally wouldn't see such low-priority patients. However, Dr. Hsu had grown weary of Simon's poor performance on the job of late—a direct result of his spending every waking hour, and not a few of his sleeping ones, in his increasingly futile quest to find out what the hell was happening to his sister—and so had shoved him rather low on the hospital's totem pole.

"So you're the infamous Simon Tam," Garcia said.

"I wasn't aware that I was infamous. Or famous, for that matter."

"Walk in the right circles, Doc, and you most surely are. Same for your lovely sister."

Simon almost dropped his stethoscope. "What about my sister?"

"You ain't the only one has relatives in the academy, Doc. How-some-ever, you *are* the only one with, shall we say, disposable income."

Frowning, Simon asked, "What's that supposed to mean?"

Garcia suddenly got up off the exam bed. "My stomach's feeling a damn sight better, Doc. Thanks for your care. If you find yourself at the Moonshuttle

Bar & Grill 'round midnight or so, I'll buy you a drink."

With that, he left.

— —

The Moonshuttle was a dreary little tavern tucked in a forgotten corner of Capital City, buried beneath the huge spires that extended to the clouds and beyond. Two years ago, Simon would never have set foot in a place this disgusting. Now, though, he had gone to far worse locales in his search for River, and whoever these people were, they knew that making a low-priority appointment at the hospital would get them in to see Simon. That meant they had ways of getting information from inside Alliance facilities.

Simon found Garcia in a corner stall with two other people, a man and a woman. "I believe you owe me a drink," Simon said as he approached.

"Sit a spell, Doc," Garcia said with a smile. "These are my friends, B—"

"Don't bother to introduce yourselves," Simon said as he took a seat next to the woman and opposite Garcia and the other man. "I already know that Guillermo Garcia is a ninety-six-year-old man who lives in Shomen Heights and hasn't visited a hospital since he got a new kidney ten years ago. Oh, and he has no history of gastric trouble."

Garcia—or whoever he was—smiled. "You ain't as dumb as you look, Doc."

Smiling, Simon said, "Well, I really couldn't be. You said you had information about my sister?"

28

"Yup. See, we represent us a group of people who aren't overburdened with patience regarding the Alliance."

"Independents. Didn't you already lose the war?"

Garcia made a face. "Any of us wearin' any brown coats, Doc? Naw, we ain't no damn Independents. See, fightin' the Alliance is a fool's game. What we do is work underneath it. The straight and narrow ain't so beneficial as workin' outside the law."

Simon was losing patience. "What does any of this have to do—"

Pointing at the woman next to Simon, Garcia said, "Martina here, she's got herself a son at that place where they brung your sister." He indicated the man next to him with his head. "Stanislaus here, he got a wife in there. Me, I ain't got no one, but these two folks been by my side most'a my adult life, and I don't reckon to see 'em hurt none. Now we have the means to get someone on the inside to work an escape—what we don't have is—"

"Disposable income." Simon saw where this was going. "You need money to get what you want."

"It's what everyone at this table wants, Doc. Now, you in?"

THE ACADEMY

Dr. Philbert Mathias wished the government inspector would go away.

The work they were doing with the children was incredibly delicate, and having some government goon standing over his shoulder while he and his technicians worked was simply irritating as all get-out. It was a living example of Heisenberg's uncertainty principle—that which is observed is changed by the act of observation. His presence here was tainting the results of their tests. *Why can't they just read my reports and be satisfied with that?*

Of course, Mathias was not foolish enough to say any of that out loud. One did not mouth such words in front of a government inspector if one wished to keep one's high-paying government job examining young people with impressive minds.

Right now, they were working on River Tam, who slept in one of the dream chairs, which was in the center of the room in an inclined position. Injector needles had been placed at different parts of Tam's cranium in order to stimulate different areas of her brain.

"She's dreaming." Technician Siegal gave the report while standing at one of the monitoring stations.

Next to him, Technician Waits asked, "Nightmare?"

Siegal nodded. "Off the charts. Scary monsters."

Mathias had to bite back a rebuke at such unscientific terminology. Were the inspector not here, he would have let Siegal have it, but he wanted to create the impression that he ran a tight ship here. "Let's amp it up," he said, making a notation on his clipboard. "Delcium, eight-drop."

He looked over at the inspector. The man had a pitiless face, showing no emotion whatsoever, and carried an eagle-crested baton that served no obvious function, except to scare people into thinking he would use it.

"See," he said to the inspector, "most of our best work is done when they're asleep. We can monitor and direct their subconscious, implant suggestions . . ."

Tam convulsed, which caused the inspector's eyes to briefly widen.

Smiling gently, Mathias said, "It's a little startling to see, but the results are spectacular. Especially in this case. River Tam is our star pupil."

The inspector nodded. "I've heard that."

"She's a genius. Her mental capacity is extraordinary, even with the side effects." Mathias winced, wishing he could call the words back. Mention of the side effects always provoked irrelevant questions about the nature of those side effects, and Mathias was well and truly sick of justifying what was a necessary part of the process.

Sure enough, the inspector made a request. "Tell me about them."

Mathias held in a sigh of annoyance, which would surely displease the inspector. "Well, obviously, she's unstable. The neural stripping gives them heightened cognitive reception, but it also destabilizes their own reality matrix. It manifests as borderline schizophrenia, which at this point is the price for being truly psychic."

"What use do we have for a psychic if she's insane?"

Again, Mathias held back the sigh, but it was more of a struggle this time. He'd already answered this question when the parliament had come by to see the "academy students." In fact, this inspector's presence in light of that visit by the parliament was more than a little insulting. "I don't have to tell you the security potential of someone who can read minds. And she has lucid periods—we hope to improve upon the—" *Oh, the hell with this.* "I'm sorry, sir, I have to ask if there's some reason for this inspection."

The inspector turned to look at Mathias with his brutal gaze. "Am I making you nervous?"

Hell, yes! "Key members of parliament have personally observed this subject. I was told their support for the project was unanimous. The demonstration of her power—"

Turning his back on Mathias, the inspector looked at Tam again. "How is she physically?"

At that, Mathias smiled, as this was one element of the project that had gone beyond expectations. "Like nothing we've seen. All our subjects are conditioned for combat, but River—she's a creature of extraordinary grace."

"Yes. She always did love to dance."

Mathias didn't like the sound of that. Up until that last sentence, the inspector had been speaking in an almost-bored monotone. But just then he sounded—wistful?

And how the hell does he know that she loves to dance?

The inspector dropped to one knee and slammed his eagle baton on the ground.

One and a half seconds later, Mathias's world went blank.

—

Thank you, Garcia, Simon thought as the bouncing betty disguised as an eagle exploded, sending a wave of energy through the room at about neck level. It rendered Mathias and his two flunkies unconscious in an instant, just as Garcia had promised.

He rushed to the massive chair on which River lay sleeping.

It had taken all of Simon's self-control to keep himself from reacting to seeing River for the first time in over two years—and worse, to see her full of tubes and needles, like someone who had just had a brain operation. For all he knew, she had—based on what Mathias told him, he wouldn't put anything past these butchers. He hadn't the chance to discover the extent of what they did to her, and now he wouldn't, as his window of opportunity to get himself and River out of there was closing rapidly.

Garcia had said that if Simon provided the money, he and his friends would do the rest, and they had. Simon had no idea whose uniform this was he was wearing, or whose credentials had let him in the door, but they were good enough to enable him to see Dr. Mathias on the pretense of a surprise inspection.

Gently removing the probes from River's head, he then reached into his briefcase and pulled out some swabs to stop the bleeding. "River," he whispered, "wake up. Please, it's Simon. River. It's your brother. Wake up!"

Miraculously, she started to stir. Satisfied with that, and that the bleeding from the tiny cuts made by the probes had stopped, Simon then ran to the door, removing his inspector's uniform to reveal an orderly's tunic that looked just like the one worn by the two flunkies unconscious on the floor. He heard footsteps.

"Simon."

At that, Simon almost jumped out of his skin. River had somehow appeared next to him without his hearing her. True, she was in her bare feet, and she always had moved quietly, but still . . .

"They know you've come." She spoke with more certainty than Simon had ever heard from her.

"I know," he said with a nod. "Come on."

They went out into the corridor, which was blessedly empty. The other students were nowhere to be found, and Simon couldn't spend the time looking.

"We can't make it to the surface from inside." Before he could say anything else, he heard footsteps. *That room had to be monitored, so that's probably the guards wondering why the government inspector just knocked out a doctor and two technicians and sprung a student.* "Find a—"

Before he could finish that instruction to River, his sister had scampered up over some lab equipment to the corridor's ceiling. Her legs apart in a balletic split, she wedged herself against the ceiling with her feet pressed against the molding in the corners of the walls, and held on to a sprinkler for additional support.

Mathias wasn't kidding about her grace.

The doors then opened to reveal, not guards, but two more doctors, who didn't even acknowledge Simon's presence. Simon had never understood the dismissive arrogance that most of his fellow physicians had toward medical employees who weren't doctors, but he had never shared it—which was probably why he tended to get along better with the nurses and medtechs than the other doctors.

Right now, though, he was grateful for it, as the pair ignored him and didn't notice River on the ceiling.

Once they were gone, River leapt back down, and they headed for a ventilation shaft. Only fifteen feet by fifteen feet, the shaft went all the way up through the various levels of the underground complex to the surface, and down past Simon's ability to see. He wondered if it went all the way to the planet's molten core.

Opening the window that led to the shaft, Simon and River got in. As River started climbing up, Simon closed the window and wedged it shut with his baton.

This proved wise, as two guards were running toward the shaft. They fired at the glass with their sidearms, but the lasers of course had no effect. Simon was amazed they wasted the magazines' power on a surface that they had to know was laser-proof.

Touching a button on a remote control, Simon then looked up to see the ship waiting for him at the top of the shaft that helped provide air for the academy. The shaft had been opened by Simon before he arrived, and now a hatch on the bottom of his ship extended down to where they were in the ventilation shaft.

When it stopped a foot over River's head, Simon shouted, "Get on!" The guards were now hitting the glass, and starting to crack it, brute force accomplishing what laser heat could not.

Simon touched the button again, and the panel rose back up to the one-person ship. Once inside, he instructed the computer to take off. Government inspectors traveled in one-person ships, so the only place for River was the cryo chamber in the cargo compartment. Simon managed to convince River to strip down and get into it. Once he rendezvoused with Garcia, he would be able to be a simple doctor traveling with precious cargo—which would be far easier than traveling with a girl of dubious sanity who'd just been sprung from a government facility.

River got into the chamber without complaint—though she talked plenty, and Simon understood precisely none of it. He then set course for the rendezvous with Garcia, who would dispose of the craft and take Simon and the chamber to Persephone.

If all went according to plan, the scan-proof hull that was standard equipment on an inspector's ship would keep anyone from following Simon.

"From there," Garcia had said, "you find yourself a ship that'll take you as far from the central planets as you can get." Then he had grinned. "Hell, you might be well off to go to Reaver country."

At the time, Simon had dismissed that notion, not believing in Reavers.

Persephone's Eavesdown Docks were full of ships looking to take on passengers. Simon had a wealth of choices, but ultimately, he had gone with a vessel called *Serenity,* which was headed for Boros. There were several motivating factors, not the least of which was that the ship, a battered old *Firefly*-class cargo carrier that had seen better decades, looked suffi-ciently disreputable. The Alliance would never expect a scion of the noble Tam family to be traveling on this heap.

Of course, there were other disreputable ships at Eavesdown—the challenge would've been to find a reputable one—but the young woman who was bark-ing for *Serenity* was very pretty. Simon had to confess that he hadn't expected to find anyone or anything pretty out here. Most people in the outer planets had elastic notions as to proper hygiene, and out here they didn't really have access to cosmetic enhancements that were run of the mill back home.

But this young woman—whose name, he learned,

was Kaylee—was quite pleasant to look at, even with the smudges on her face. Besides, she had a boundless enthusiasm that Simon—facing a life as a fugitive far away from everything he'd ever known—found comforting.

Kaylee was the ship's mechanic. The rest of the crew included the pilot, Hoban Washburne—whom everyone called "Wash"—his wife Zoë Washburne, who served as first mate, and Jayne Cobb, who—well, Simon wasn't sure what his function was, though he apparently excelled at violence. One of *Serenity*'s two shuttles was rented to a licensed Companion named Inara Serra. One of the most beautiful women Simon had ever met, she also brought an air of legitimacy to *Serenity* that might have driven Simon to another ship, but he had already committed to Kaylee, and paid her half the transport fee. That fee took up most of his remaining money, and he'd never be able to afford to switch to another ship now.

Two other passengers came onto *Serenity* with Simon: a shepherd named Derrial Book and a civilian named Lawrence Dobson. The captain—Malcolm Reynolds, a barely polite man who practically had the word SCOUNDREL tattooed on his forehead—told them that they would be detouring to Whitefall first.

That, however, proved the least of Simon Tam's problems. The scan-proof hull hadn't done as well as he'd hoped, as an Alliance agent was waiting for them at Eavesdown: Dobson, who had instructions to take River back to the academy, instructions he followed through on while *Serenity* was in space.

In the end, though, Dobson was taken care of, and after a harrowing adventure involving Reavers—who surprised Simon by being terribly real—and Captain Reynolds prematurely thawing River, Simon was invited to stay on *Serenity* as her medic. Simon had operated on Kaylee when Dobson shot her, saving her life, which did a lot to mollify Mal.

Later, Simon learned that Mal and Zoë had fought in the war, on the Independent side, so they had no great love for the Alliance either. Harboring Alliance fugitives was a hardship for them, but one that Mal seemed willing to bear in exchange for a good medic.

Over the past two years, he'd learned that his own family could barely be called that. But on *Serenity*, even with all the dangers—Mal and his crew led a hard life, and Dobson wasn't the only Alliance agent who was out to get them—he and River had actually found a home. Simon had even brought them one of their jobs, the robbery of a hospital on Ariel. It enabled Simon to do a proper scan of River's brain, and he'd been able to make use of Garcia by having Jayne use him to get fake IDs for the hospital so the *Serenity* crew could loot it of drugs and medications.

Things had changed, of course. Both Inara and Shepherd Book had moved on, the former to a Companion outpost, the latter to settle down with the miners on Haven. But still, River loved the ship and the crew, and occasionally, Simon found himself able to consider the possibility of actual happiness.

He wondered how long it would last.

The Story:
EIGHT YEARS
AFTER THE WAR

LILAC

For Malcolm Reynolds, today was a good day.

Serenity was still flying. They had a job, one that would pay a decent amount of coin. That job was taking them to the moon Lilac, over which *Serenity* had pulled into orbit, and into the atmosphere of which *Serenity* was now descending, with the ever-reliable Wash at the helm. Right now, Mal was standing behind Wash, who had his firm hand on the boat's controls. *Serenity* was a multipurpose craft, able to function as well in atmo as in the black, which was a fair piece of the reason why Mal bought her seven years back.

Yes, today was a good day.

Then something ripped off the nose of the ship and flew up and away into the stratosphere at a great rate, at which point Mal's day got a bit worse.

"What was that?" he asked Wash.

Wash's eyes grew wide. "Whoa! Did you see *that?*"

Serenity then bucked a bit, more than it should have with the aforementioned steady hand at the controls. Mal did not see Wash waver in the slightest, which meant that the piece that went flying off was, sad to say, *just* what he thought it was.

"Was that the primary buffer panel?"

Wash swallowed. "It did seem to resemble—"

Mal was in no mood for equivocation. "Did the primary buffer panel just fall off my gorram ship for no apparent reason?"

The ship bucked again. Mal thought to bend his knees and keep from falling over, which enabled him to keep a portion of his dignity. Since he was rapidly losing all portions of his temper, this kept things in a kind of balance.

Meekly, Wash said, "Looks like."

"I thought Kaylee checked our entry couplings," Mal said testily. "I have a very clear memory of it."

Wash probably would've shrugged, if not for the white-knuckle grip he had on the controls. "Yeah, well, if she doesn't give us some extra flow from the engine room to offset the burn-through, this landing is gonna get pretty interesting."

Mal shook his head, having only understood half of what Wash was saying. The reason why he kept Wash and Kaylee around was so they could understand all the technical *go-se,* freeing him up to do captain-y things. "Define *interesting.*"

Calmly, Wash said, " 'Oh God, oh God, we're all gonna die'?"

Restraining himself from killing Wash only because the pilot had the best chance of landing Mal's boat in fewer than ten pieces, Mal instead grabbed the 'com unit that would transmit his voice to all of *Serenity.* "This is the captain. There's a little problem with our entry sequence. We may experience slight turbulence and then explode." He cut the connection and then looked at Wash. "Can you shave the vector—"

"I'm doing it! It's not enough," Wash said in a tone indicating disappointment that his captain had so little confidence in him. For his part, Mal could live with Wash's disappointment, though if he didn't pull a miracle out of the pocket of the blessedly ugly shirt he was wearing, Mal wasn't going to live with it for very long.

Loosening his grip on the controls, Wash hit the intercom and called out, "Kaylee!"

Moving toward the exit, Mal said, "Just get us on the ground!"

"That part'll happen, pretty definitely."

Thus brimming with confidence, Mal left the bridge and went down the stairs to the crew quarters corridor, just as Jayne Cobb was climbing up out of his bunk.

Mal didn't like Jayne very much, but liking wasn't a particularly critical component of their relationship. He first came across Jayne about two years earlier, when *Serenity* was doing a job on Caliban. On the other side of the job was a gent name of Marco Ferlinghetti who had the brains of a cabbage—and that was only if one was feeling inhospitable toward vegetable matter. Mal had figured to be able to run rings around Marco, so it was something of a surprise when Marco and his two thugs were pointing guns at Mal and Zoë right outside *Serenity*.

It didn't take long to suss out that it was one of the thugs, a bruiser by the name of Jayne Cobb, who actually got the drop on them. Mal immediately offered him a job, promising him a bigger cut and better accommodations than Marco was giving him if he switched sides. Jayne, who had a pretty direct view of the 'verse—mostly that he preferred a state of affairs that benefited Jayne Cobb—took the deal.

Having Jayne on board had worked out well for Mal, and not just because Jayne declining the offer would likely have left Mal and Zoë with a bad case of dead. Jayne was definitely someone you wanted by your side in a hairy situation, and since Mal's life more or less consisted of going from one hairy situation to the next, that proved beneficial. Mind, you never wanted Jayne at your back, as there was no telling when he'd get it in his head to stab you in it.

Right now, Jayne wasn't going to be stabbing anybody, mostly by way of being armed to the teeth with various and sundry projectile weaponry, as well as a bandolier full of grenades.

"We're gonna explode?" Jayne asked. "I don't wanna explode."

A *very* direct view of the 'verse. "Jayne, how many weapons you plan on bringing?" Mal asked. "You only got the two arms."

"I just get excitable as to choice—like to have my options open."

"I don't plan on any shooting taking place during this job."

Jayne glowered at him. "Well, what you plan and what takes place ain't ever exactly been similar."

Mal found he couldn't really argue with that. Still,

he felt the need to show some vestige of captain-y authority, so he said, "No grenades." When Jayne groaned, he repeated himself: *"No* grenades!"

On the far end of the hallway, Zoë came into the corridor, having come up from the cargo deck on the lower level. "Are we crashing again?" she asked, sounding almost bored.

"Talk to your husband. Is the mule prepped?"

"Good to go, sir. Just loading her up."

Mal nodded and moved off toward the engine room.

Zoë, meanwhile, looked at Jayne and his armament—which currently took up more space than Jayne his own self. "Are those grenades?"

Sulking now, Jayne said, "Cap'n doesn't want 'em."

"We're robbing the place; we're not occupying it."

Jayne's response was lost to Mal as he ran through the dining room, pausing to grab a dumpling that someone had left on the table. The boat shook again as he bit down on it, causing Mal to come within a hair of biting his tongue. *That'd be a perfect end to the day,* he thought angrily, and shouted, "Kaylee!"

Going through the far door, Mal then went down another corridor to Kaylee's domain. The engine room was dominated by a giant motor that spun at a great rate—the faster it spun, the more power *Serenity* used in propulsion. At least, that was what Mal assumed—he honestly had no clue what any of the parts did or where they went. Aside from a catalyzer, at least, and he knew *that* one only because Kaylee showed him once and he was soon thereafter forced to install it himself by virtue of being the only one on the ship when the replacement was acquired. To add injury to insult, he was bleeding badly from a belly wound while doing it. He rightly supposed that he'd go to his grave remembering exactly how to install a catalyzer.

The rest of it, though, was beyond him, which was why he often felt Kaylee was the most valuable member of the crew. She hadn't been on *Serenity* for more than half an hour before she fixed a problem that had kept her grounded for days—this without ever having gone up in a *Firefly*-class boat before. "Natural talent," she called it. Kaylee had been brought on board by Bester, her predecessor, who had taken advantage of Mal's lack of engineering knowledge to get himself a job for which he was completely unqualified. Within minutes of her repair job, Kaylee was the new mechanic and Bester was unemployed.

"Kaylee," he said to the young woman now as she dashed back and forth with tools and things, "what in the sphincter of hell are you playing at? We got the primary buffer—"

"Everything's shiny, Cap'n." As always, Kaylee had a happy smile on her face. "Not to fret."

Mal, however, was in something of a fretting mood. "You told me—" *Serenity* jolted again; Mal braced himself against the door frame. "You told me the entry couplings would hold for another week!"

Without looking up from her work, Kaylee said, "That was six months ago, Cap'n."

First Wash, then Jayne, now Kaylee. My whole crew is like to snark me today, if we live long enough. Again, he gathered the shards of his captain-y dignity.

"My ship don't crash. If she crashes, *you* crashed her."

Kaylee simply went about her work, even as steam came shooting out of somewhere.

Realizing that he was simply distracting the mechanic, Mal turned to leave, only to see Simon Tam in the hallway.

"Doctor," he said, walking away from the engine room. "Guess I need to get innocked 'fore we hit planetside." *Assuming we don't hit it as hard as I fear.* The ship then jolted again. "Bit of a rockety ride. Nothing to worry about."

"I'm not worried." Indeed, Simon didn't sound worried. But then, he'd been on the ship a fair piece, so he knew Wash's skills.

"Fear is nothing to be ashamed of, Doc."

"This isn't fear, this is anger."

Mal laughed. "Well, it's kinda hard to tell the one from the other, face like yours."

"I imagine if it were fear, my eyes would be wider."

"I'll look for that next time."

Then, finally, the doc got to the point, which came to Mal as a kindness. "You're not taking her."

Or maybe not so much of a kindness. He walked past Simon. "No, no, that's not a thing I'm interested in talking over with—"

"She's not going with you—that's *final!*"

Yup, the whole crew's gonna snark me, youbetcha. Exceptin' Zoë, of course, but she at least has a fair understanding of comportment. Might need to give a refresher in that, once the job's done. He turned back to Simon. "I hear the words 'that's final' come out of your mouth ever again, they truly will be." He turned back around and headed down the corridor. "This is *my* boat. Y'all are guests on it."

"Guests? I earn my passage, Captain."

Mal had to silently admit that was so. In fact, when Mal had come back to Jiangyin to rescue him and River from some rather backwards-thinking folk, Simon had asked why they came back. Mal told him that they were part of his crew. He meant it then, so why was he calling him a guest now?

The answer came fairly quickly: It annoyed the young doctor, and annoying the young doctor gave Mal amusement, which frankly was in short supply today.

He said, "And it's time your little sister learned from your fine example."

"I've earned my passage treating bullet holes, knife wounds, laser burns—"

"Some of our jobs are trickier than others," Mal said with a shrug as he walked past the guest quarters, including the rooms River and Simon still used and the one Shepherd Book had since abandoned.

"And you want to put my sister in the middle of that?"

"Didn't say 'want'—said 'will.' It's one job, Doc. She'll be fine."

They walked through to the infirmary. The place had been well stocked when Mal bought the boat, but was lacking for a proper caretaker until Simon came along. He had the place in even better shape now.

As Simon prepared a hypo, Mal said, "She's a

reader. Sees into the truth of things. Might see trouble before it's coming—which is of use to me."

"And that's your guiding star, isn't it? What's of use?"

Again, Mal laughed. "Honestly, Doctor, I think we may really crash this time anyway."

Simon jabbed the inoculation into Mal's arm with a bit more force than was necessary—but probably as much as was warranted, given the hard time Mal was giving the boy.

"Do you understand what I've gone through to keep River away from the Alliance?"

"I do, and it's a fact we here have been courteous enough to keep to our own selves."

Finally, Simon's face changed expression, and this time Mal really did see fear. "Are you threatening to—"

Mal had had enough of this. "I look out for me and mine. That don't include you 'less I conjure it does. Now you stuck a thorn in the Alliance's paw, and that tickles me a bit, but it also means I gotta step twice as fast to avoid them, and that means turning down plenty of jobs. Even honest ones." His shot given, Mal exited the infirmary. Simon followed. "Every year since the war, the Alliance pushes further out, fences off another piece of the 'verse." Unbidden, the smell of dead soldiers lining the blood-soaked ground of Serenity Valley invaded his nostrils; as always, Mal forced the memories into the dark corner where he preferred they stay. "Come a day there won't be room for naughty men like us to slip about at all. This job goes south, there well may not be another." They came out into the massive cargo deck. "So here is us, on the raggedy edge. Don't push me, and I won't push you, *dong le ma?*"

Simon said nothing, but instead moved up the metal stairs to the catwalk that encircled the cargo area on the second deck. Mal shook his head and walked over to the new mule.

This was Mal's pride and joy. A while back, they got their hands on one of the few remaining Lassiters, one of the early laser pistols. Expensive as hell, they'd lifted it from right under the nose of a rich gent name of Durran from his estate on Bellerophon. Took a spell to find a buyer for so major an item, but a buyer they did find, and the funds went to purchase a fancy new mule. The previous one, which was strictly a ground vehicle, had been damaged a fair piece during a raid on a skyplex owned by a fella name of Niska. Kaylee had done her best to patch it up, but it never worked right after they set off a passel of grenades in it. Mal couldn't really complain overmuch, seeing as how the raid was a rescue of Mal himself from Niska, who was torturing Mal pretty badly. Besides which, though the new mule wasn't cheap, it was an air vehicle, and therefore of considerable more use than the old one.

Serenity jolted again, and Mal looked at Zoë, who was, along with Jayne, loading up the mule with various duffel bags. "Zoë, is Wash gonna straighten this boat out before we get flattened?"

Zoë smirked. "Like a downy feather, sir. Nobody flies like my mister."

Before Mal could make a disparaging remark about how feathers can still come to a bad end if they fall from far enough in the sky, he felt the deckplates push up against his boots, indicating that *Serenity* was slowing down.

Moments later, they gently touched ground. Mal barely felt it.

Walking over to the intercom, Mal tapped it with the back of his hand. "Not a bad landin' there, Wash."

"Told you we'd hit the ground, Mal."

"That you did." Mal should never have lost confidence. If you taped two wings to a brick, Wash could break atmo with it and have it orbiting your moon inside of five minutes. "Keep it turnin' over—I expect we'll be fixin' to make a quick exit."

"Will do."

Zoë handed him a pair of goggles. "You'll need these, sir."

Mal sighed. "I have to wear 'em?"

"No, sir—you don't 'have' to do anything. That's one of the perks of being captain."

"So I can leave the goggles?" Mal was grateful for this. The goggles made him look silly. Jayne had put his on, and he looked *powerful* silly, which, given that Jayne was one of the scarier individuals Mal had gotten to know personally, was going some.

"Of course, sir. I'll just make sure to put aside some of our loot for the seeing-eye dog you'll need when the grit in the air tears your eyes out."

Snatching the goggles out of Zoë's hands, Mal said, "Fine, I'll wear 'em. But I'll look like an idiot."

"I should think you'd be used to that, sir."
So much for keeping Zoë off the snark list.

--

Simon Tam walked up the stairs to the catwalk, where he found River lying on her side. Unlike when he saw her in the academy, she looked peaceful, wearing a pretty summer dress, and barefoot. He knelt down by her side. "River?"

Her eyes opened. "I know. We're going for a ride."

"I suppose that's one way of looking at it," he muttered. He had feared this day ever since a bounty hunter named Jubal Early had infiltrated *Serenity,* and come close to succeeding, not only in taking River and Simon, but killing the rest of the crew. It had been River who saved them all, then. Shortly before that, Kaylee revealed that River had shot three of Niska's thugs back at his skyplex without even looking at them.

Over the months on this vessel, he had come to learn that Mal Reynolds was a person who made use of whatever resources were available to him, and River was rapidly proving herself to be such a resource. Objectively, he probably would have admitted that Mal had a point, but it was also completely impossible for him to be objective where River was concerned. She had been his only source of joy throughout a childhood that, looking back on it, was otherwise pretty miserable. He threw away everything that he had thought to be important to save her from Mathias and his goons, and he was not going to just let Mal take her on a damn job!

Except, of course, he was.

River padded down the stairs, the epitome of grace, her bare feet hardly seeming to touch the metal stairs. Simon grabbed her boots and followed her down, his own shoes making clanking noises as he went.

When they got to the cargo level, Jayne was tossing a disturbing amount of spare ammunition into the spaces on the mule between its four seats. The cargo door was opened, having unfolded into a ramp that took one from the ship to the ground. Zoë handed River a set of goggles even as Simon gave her her boots. She took the goggles, but not the footwear.

Having given in to the inevitable, Simon looked at his sister. "Now, River, you stay behind the others. If there's fighting, you drop to the floor—or run away. It's okay to leave them to die."

River put the goggles on—they took up half her small face, obscuring her tiny nose, and making her look like a very confused fish. "I'm the brains of the operation."

The sad thing is, that's probably true, Simon thought. Certainly Mal's own planning skills left something to be desired. Simon had always found it telling that, of the two most successful jobs *Serenity* had pulled in the time since Simon and River came on board, one was planned by Simon himself.

Zoë, Jayne, Mal, and River were all climbing into the mule. Zoë was saying, "We should hit town right during Sunday worship. Won't be any crowds."

Lovely, Simon thought, *robbing people during their time of worship. I wonder what Shepherd Book would have to say.* Simon wondered if his growing unease lately related to the departure of the shepherd. Book had always been a voice of reason and steady counsel. So, for that matter, had been Inara. *What kind of universe lets them leave but keeps Jayne on board?*

Mal said, "If Fanty and Mingo are right about the payroll, this could look to be a sunny day for us."

Simon winced at the pun. He approached Mal. "Captain, I'll ask you one last time—"

Naturally, Mal wouldn't hear a word of it. "Doctor, I'm taking your sister under my protection here." Simon found that statement wholly unreassuring. "If anything happens to her, anything at all, I swear to you I will get *very* choked up. Honestly. There could be tears."

With that, the mule lifted off the deck and zipped out through the cargo door.

Kaylee—whose presence Simon hadn't even registered, which right there told him how distracted this whole thing had made him—sidled up to Simon. "Don't mind the captain none, Simon. I know he'll look out for her."

Mal's intentions were of much less concern to Simon than Mal's results, and history didn't paint a pretty picture. "It's amazing. I bring River all the way out to the raggedy edge of the 'verse so she can hide from the Alliance by *robbing banks.*"

"It's just a little trading station," Kaylee said in her

ever-cheery voice. "They'll be back 'fore you can spit. Not that you spit . . ."

Simon found that he couldn't deal with Kaylee's perpetual good mood at the moment, as it was likely to be infectious—and he wanted to hang onto his bad mood a little while longer.

Besides, he was still holding River's boots, and he felt like an idiot. So he stormed off, leaving Kaylee behind. He promised himself to apologize to her later. Right now, he wanted to go to the infirmary and prepare for the inevitable casualties. Over the months since he signed on, he'd done more trauma surgery than he had in the previous three years working in Capital City Hospital, from bullet wounds and stab wounds to reattaching Mal's ear after Niska cut it off. Somehow, he had a feeling that he was going to be doing more operating before this day was done.

He prayed fervently that it wouldn't be River he was performing the surgery on.

——

The wind whipped through Jayne Cobb's close-cropped hair and tickled the hairs of his goatee. He felt naked, somehow, probably because of the lack of grenades. There were times when he just didn't get the cap'n and Zoë. Folk like Wash and the pretty-boy doc were one thing—he didn't expect them to appreciate the fine and noble ways of violence—but Mal and Zoë were soldiers. Fought in a gorram war and everything.

So why won't they let me bring no ruttin' grenades?

Jayne sighed. It was all water under whatever it was that water went under now. He'd just have to make do with half a dozen guns, which always served him well in a pinch.

As they settled the mule in next to the trading post, Jayne looked around at the single town that made up the entire populated area of this here *chou ma niao* moon. The buildings looked like they were put together by someone who was blind, stupid, or both—wood, adobe, metal, plastic, all of it went into the building. *People this dumb deserve to get their money took. Assuming they have any.*

Jayne turned to Mal while Zoë tethered the mule. "What are we hoping to find here that equals the worth of a turd?"

"Security payroll," Mal said. "Alliance don't have the manpower to 'enforce the peace' on every border moon cluster. They hire out to the private firms, who will *not* work for credit."

Jayne smiled. He appreciated that particular rule of thumb.

Mal continued. "They get paid in cashy money, which once a month rests here."

Frowning, Jayne saw what he feared was a critical flaw in Mal's plan. "Don't that lead back to the Alliance anyhow?"

Zoë answered that one. "No private firm would ever report a theft of its own payroll. They'd appear weak, might lose their contract."

Jayne supposed he saw the sense in that.

"We're as ghosts in this," Mal said. "Won't but rattle the floor."

"Shiny." Jayne cocked his gun. "Let's be bad guys."

Mal turned to River, whose presence on this particular journey remained a puzzle to Jayne. "You ready to go to work, darlin'?"

The crazy girl had been staring at the ground. She looked up at Mal. "There's no pattern to the pebbles here. They're completely random. I tried to count them, but you drove too fast. Hummingbird."

"Right." Mal just stared at her for a second. "Great. Let's go."

And that was one of her more lucid-like conversations. I done told Mal not to bring the crazy girl along. One of these days, Mal's gonna actually listen to me, and that will be a day in which I will bet real money that I don't get shot at or stabbed. He still recalled the time River slashed at him with a knife, and that was not what he'd call a fond remembrance.

Mal and Jayne burst into the trading station, weapons at the ready, Zoë, also armed, right behind, River behind her looking small and scared like usual. *Maybe she'll get her crazy head shot off.*

Heartened by this thought, Jayne ran into the station, which looked like it combined general store with post office with bank. Typical all-purpose commercial enterprise for tiny-ass towns on tiny-ass moons like this. There were about a dozen or so folk, most of them looking to be dirt-poor. *Good thing they ain't the ones we robbing.*

Zoë shot out the only visible security camera, which had the dual effect of killing surveillance and getting everyone's attention. Mal held up his gun toward the ceiling. "Hands and knees and heads bowed down! Everybody, *now!*"

Two damn fools tried to rush Mal, which led him to point his gun right at 'em, convincing them to stop.

Another damn fool tried to rush Jayne. Not wanting to waste a bullet on someone that stupid, Jayne clotheslined him, slamming his arm into the fool's chest. He flipped over backward. Jayne grabbed his legs and made sure the fool's head met the floor at a nice high speed. Had he a brain, Jayne suspected he would soon be suffering a certain amount of damage to it.

Mal said, "Y'all wanna be looking very intently at your own belly buttons. I see a head start to rise, violence is gonna ensue."

Jayne leaned over the fool. His chest had felt a mite harder than the average rib cage. Ripping open the fool's shirt revealed a security uniform—probably body armor. He removed a pin from the uniform. "Looks like this is the place."

Mal looked around. "You've probably guessed we mean to be thieving here, but what we are after is not yours. So let's have no undue fussing."

While Mal talked, Jayne went over to the back office. Sure enough, there was a safe. He pulled on the handle and was completely not surprised to find it didn't budge. "She's locked up."

Jayne saw River get Zoë's attention and then point at a man. Jayne looked at the man and saw that he was slowly taking a weapon out from under his belt. Zoë stuck the muzzle of her shotgun into his cheek.

Reluctantly, Jayne was starting to see a hair of wisdom in letting the crazy girl come along. Zoë wasn't what you'd call unobservant, so if this fella was catching her unawares, he had a measure of stealth and might've caused some difficulties.

To the man she had the gun on, Zoë said, "You know what the definition of a hero is? It's someone who gets other people killed. You can look it up later."

Times like this, Jayne wondered what life'd be like if he and Zoë—and, if she insisted, Wash—struck out on their own. He had a premonition that it might be a fair sight more profitable without Mal gumming up the works.

But naw, Zoë'd sooner leave Wash than not be with Mal. And truth to tell, Jayne was still doing better on *Serenity* than he ever had done elsewhere.

Meanwhile, Mal walked over to the old fella behind the counter and dragged him over to the vault. "This is just a crop moon," the old fella said. "Don't think you'll find what you—"

In a tight voice, Mal told the man, in Chinese, to shut up and make them wealthy.

Seeing the wisdom of Mal's words—or at least the wisdom of their big guns—the old fella entered a code into the keypad next to the vault. Mal then opened it right up.

Jayne had been itching to shoot someone all day, and that itch just got a lot harder not to scratch. The vault wasn't exactly empty, but it was as close as made no never mind. Maybe three bills, some scattered coin. What was in that vault would barely cover the fuel for the mule's trip to and from *Serenity.*

Zoë looked at Mal. "At last," she said dryly, "we can retire and give up this life of crime."

Thoughts of striking out on his own with Zoë returned to Jayne's mind, even as Mal suddenly reached into the vault—and pulled a lever.

A trapdoor then opened in the floor, revealing a nice big staircase leading down to a shiny metal corridor. This whole nothing town was typical outer planets: a right mess. But this corridor? Pure Alliance.

Jayne grinned.

Mal looked at the old fella. "Is there a guard down there? Be truthful."

The old fella nodded. "Y'all are Browncoats, hey? Fought for independence?"

"War's long done," Mal said. "We're all just folk now."

Of course, Jayne didn't fight in no war. Pay wasn't good enough on either side.

Yelling down the shaft, Mal said, "Listen up! We are coming down to empty that vault!"

A voice yelled back up. "You have to give me your authorization password!"

Jayne lifted his machine gun and fired two dozen rounds down the staircase.

There was a pause. Then: "Okay!"

Zoë and Mal proceeded down the stairs, leaving

Jayne to watch the moon folk and the crazy girl. *Better be some good coin down yonder.*

Minutes later, River started shouting.

— —

Since coming into the trading post, River was bored. Counting pebbles had been fun for a while, since it was such a challenge with the mule going so fast. But now that they were here, that had lost its allure.

At first, she was excited to be going on a job, to be helping in a scheme, to be aiding and abetting in the commission of a crime. Everyone else on *Serenity* got to help out. Even the Companion and the shepherd helped out here and there, before they left *Serenity,* but not River, even though she was considerably smarter than anyone else on the ship.

Of course, she was considerably crazier. She knew that. It wasn't her fault, and it wasn't their fault, it was the fault of Dr. Philbert Mathias and the other people at the academy whose names and dates of birth she could recall without any difficulty.

In fact, since she was bored, she did that, listing all the academy faculty in alphabetical order, then again in chronological order by date of birth.

That got boring pretty quickly, and reminded River too much of bad things, so she thought back further, to back when she was at elementary. One of her favorite days was the one where they were learning history in Professor Rao's class. At the time, she was only nine, but everyone else in the class was twelve—and River was a lot smarter than anyone in that class, but her parents had been cautioned against putting her any farther ahead for fear of what they called "bad socialization," which was grown-up talk for "the other kids will pick on her." Not that River cared; other kids already picked on her, but they were stupid, and she didn't care what stupid people thought.

Professor Rao started telling them about how the Alliance came about. "Earth-That-Was could no longer sustain our numbers, we were so many. We found a new solar system: dozens of planets and hundreds of moons—each one terraformed, a process taking decades, to support human life. To be new Earths. The central planets were the first settled and are the most advanced, embodying civilization at its peak. Life on the outer planets—" And here, Rao could've been talking about the very moon on which River was standing right now. "—is much more primitive and difficult. That's why the central planets formed the Alliance, so everyone can enjoy the comfort and enlightenment of true civilization. That's why we fought the War for Unification."

River, of course, had known all this years before she ever got anywhere near the class, but a lot of it was new to her older classmates. Most of them had never been out of the central planets, and were fascinated by the entire notion.

Plus they thought the war was interesting.

Songmin, one of the students, asked, "Now that the war's over, our soldiers get to come home, yes?"

"Some of them," Rao said. "Some will be stationed on the rim planets as peace enforcers."

"I don't understand," said Borodin, one of the boys, who started most of his sentences with those three words. "Why were the Independents even fighting us? Why wouldn't they *look* to be more civilized?"

"That's a good question," Rao said, even though it wasn't. "Does anybody want to open on that?"

Jeanne said, "I hear they're cannibals."

Another boy, Marvin, said, "That's only Reavers."

Hannah rolled her eyes. "Reavers aren't real."

Marvin turned back to look at Hannah. "Full well they are! They attack settlers from space, they kill them and wear their skins and rape them for hours and hours—"

"Bai duo, an jing yidian!" Rao cried, calling for silence. That got Marvin to be quiet, which always was a good thing as far as River was concerned. In a calmer voice, the professor continued: "It's true that there are—dangers on the outer planets. So let's follow up on Borodin's question. With all the social and medical advancements we can bring to the Independents, why would they fight so hard against us?"

Then River spoke up, which was the only reason why she remembered this day as one of her favorites. "We meddle."

"River?" Rao sounded surprised that she'd said anything. In Chinese, she added, "I'm sorry?"

"People don't like to be meddled with. We tell them what to do, what to think, don't run, don't walk, we're

65

in their homes and in their heads and we haven't the right. We're meddlesome."

Professor Rao hadn't liked that. She thought it was an unfair thing to say about the Alliance, and then she changed the subject.

But River was happy because she knew she was right.

Having enjoyed that memory, she once again got bored, but at least she'd passed almost half a minute. Now she looked around the trading post. She examined closely each of the fifteen people, an assortment of adults and children. In her mind, she created entire life stories for each of them—some of which were actually true, some of which she made up because it was more interesting than their real lives.

That took another thirty seconds, until she was bored again.

So she looked at her fellow thieves, her comrades in arms, her partners in crime. The thug was as brutally direct as ever. All that mattered to him was the immediate. The past was of no consequence to Jayne Cobb, and the future of even less. His mind was entirely in the here-and-now.

Zoë was both the same and different. The same in that she was simple to figure out; different in that, where Jayne was simple because there was so little to him, Zoë was simple because she was uncomplicated. She had only two foci in her mind: Malcolm Reynolds and Hoban Washburne. Nothing else mattered, except insofar as it related to the two men in her life. Not that there was any competition or conflict. Zoë's dedication to the captain was of a wholly different feel than that of her dedication to her husband. The only similarity was that she would happily die for either of them.

She would be just as happy to kill for them. That was why, even though Jayne was the most brutal person on *Serenity*, Zoë was the person who scared River the most.

At least, she was now that Shepherd Book was gone.

As for Captain Reynolds, he had a lot more to him; he was the only person River knew who lived with pain as much as River herself did. Where Jayne lived in the present, Mal lived in the past. More precisely, he lived in one particular time and place: Serenity Valley on Hera, where the last battle of the war was fought.

Mal had never left that valley. He named his ship after it so he wouldn't ever *have* to leave it. And woe be to anyone who tried to take him away from it.

Then River noticed that one of the people had the intention to shoot Zoë. He was also doing it quietly and slowly so he wouldn't get anyone's attention.

But nobody was quiet enough for River to miss, unless they were dead.

River looked at Zoë and pointed at the man. She took care of it in that way that made her so scary.

The heist was continuing on just fine without River, and now that she'd actually made a contribution, she was bored again. She'd already studied everything about the people in the post, and within three seconds, she'd memorized the room's entire layout.

So she moved outward.

As Zoë had said, most of the people of Lilac were in the local church. Based on the version of the Bible they were reading from, they were New Covenantists, a type of Christianity River had never heard of until today, but now knew everything about, including their acknowledgment of the Gnostic Gospels, but repudiation of the Book of John.

Having learned all she could learn from the church, she then noticed two people walking down the street—among the few who were neither in this post nor in the church. It was a woman and her son. The woman was carrying a bucket filled with water from a nearby well.

Jayne fired thirteen rounds of ammunition into the tunnel that Captain Reynolds had just opened. The woman and her son heard it.

"Repeater," the boy said, referring to Jayne's gun. River had never heard it called that—Jayne just called it "Phoebe."

"Did sound summat like gunblast," the woman with the bucket said. "Maybe you aught run tell lawman."

River was about to warn Jayne—the captain and Zoë had already gone down the stairs—about this potential fly in the ointment when she felt something else.

Something horrible.

She'd felt it once before, in the mind of the sole survivor of a settler transport. Only what she felt then was, she realized, a faint echo of what she felt now from the man standing behind the mother and her child.

68

Scars littered the body of the creature—River couldn't bring herself to think of this disfigured thing as a person—as did rashes from radiation poisoning. Until the boy had turned around, she hadn't noticed him for the same reason why she didn't notice dead people.

For River to know you were there, she had to feel your mind.

And Reavers didn't have much left by way of a mind.

But when they did think, it was when they killed, and this Reaver suddenly went crazy, producing a knife and slashing the woman and child to pieces.

River liked it better when she couldn't feel the Reaver, because now it was *all* she could feel, the ugliness, the brutality, the nihilism, the sheer, unmitigated, unbridled terror that made Jayne's brutality seem like Wash's gentleness.

She screamed.

Until Jayne grabbed her shoulder, she hadn't realized that she had fallen to the floor of the post. "What the hell is up?" Jayne asked. "You all right? What's goin' on?"

Jayne was simple, it was true, and so River had only to force herself to whisper one word to provide all the warning that would be required:

"Reavers."

--

When Fanty and Mingo had sold Mal on this job, one of the features he'd been anticipating was that the money would be guarded by someone very much like this young'un he and Zoë encountered near the vault. The type who liked the idea of being in law enforcement a lot more than the reality. Mal suspected that the boy had applied to be a fed and failed—or might've simply realized that it was a line of work featuring a lot more danger than it did reward. So instead, he took a job with a security firm, which allowed a man to puff himself up a ways, guarding and the like, without ever having to worry about, say, getting shot.

Well, *mostly* ever. Excepting those times when thieves come to take your payroll.

Mal was happy to see the guard being all reasonable-like with regard to Mal's proposition that they steal the money, which he suspected was mostly the result of Jayne's little display of gunfire. He opened the vault with minimal hesitation—certainly a fair piece less so than the old man upstairs—and then, while Zoë relieved the vault of its contents, made an interesting request.

"I think, sir, it'd be best if'n you shoot me."

This amused Mal. "You *want* me to shoot you?"

"Yes, sir, I surely do, sir."

"You do understand, don't you, son, that the object of you givin' me this here cash is to relieve yourself of the opportunity to get shot?"

"Yes, sir, but I believe that my employers will find my craven succumbin' to that concession to be sufficient cause to terminate my employ. However, if I find myself with a convincin' wound, I might be able to plead extenuatin' circumstances."

Smiling, Mal said, "I believe I can abide that

70

request. Just leaves the question of where. Leg's good. It'll bleed plenty, and we avoid any necessary organs."

Now the guard was wincing. "I was thinkin' more of a graze . . ."

"Well, you don't want it to look like you just gave up."

Nodding, the guard said, "No, I get tha—"

"Mal!"

Gritting his teeth at the sudden shout, Mal wondered if Jayne would ever avail himself of the opportunity to grow a brain. "Every heist," he muttered, "he's gotta start yelling my name."

Jayne came barreling down the stairs, passing Zoë, who was on the way up with the loot. "Mal! Reavers!"

A fist of ice closed over Mal's heart. He'd had more than one encounter with Reavers in his time, and he chalked up his still being among the breathing to be the dumbest of dumb luck.

Jayne was still carrying on. "The girl's pitchin' a fit! They're here, or they're comin' soon!"

"Get on the mule," he said to Jayne.

Nodding, Jayne grabbed some bags and ran back up the stairs.

Mal turned to the guard, who looked confused. The boy probably thought the Reavers just to be bedtime stories. The young doctor thought much the same right up until a Reaver damn near took 'em at Whitefall a ways back. Pointing at the vault door, he asked, "Does that open from the inside?"

"Uh, yes."

Putting on his sergeant voice, the one he always

used to get the troops' attention during the war, Mal said, "You get everyone upstairs in there, and you *seal* it. Long as you got air, you don't open up, you understand?"

The guard's mouth moved, and sounds came out of his mouth, but none of it was remarkable for its coherence.

Mal got right in the boy's face. "Get them inside the vault!"

Nodding so rapidly, Mal feared the boy's head would come off, the guard then ran upstairs. Mal followed. Jayne and Zoë made for the door. River was lying on the floor, whispering a string of nonsense that was impressive even by her high standards. Mal caught the words *knife, skin, dead,* and, yes, *Reaver* amidst the gibberish.

Reaching down, Mal picked her up, carrying her light-as-the-air self to the door. Behind him, the guard was urging people to go down to hide in the vault.

Carrying the still-babbling River, Mal ran out to the mule, which Zoë and Jayne were hurriedly loading. "Zoë, take the wheel."

Zoë nodded, untethered the mule, and hopped into the pilot seat. Mal handed River up to Jayne, who set her down with surprising gentleness. "You see 'em?" Jayne asked. "Anybody see 'em?"

Shaking his head, Mal looked around. He didn't see anything, but he also had learned the hard way to trust River's instincts about these things. She'd been right a considerable portion more than she'd been wrong— not difficult, as she'd yet to *be* wrong—which was why Mal had the notion to take her along in the first place.

Hopping into the mule as Zoë started it up, Mal saw that River was still carrying on. "The world is on fire, but we don't care. The pain is everywhere, but we don't care."

Then the man who tried to pull a gun on Zoë came bursting out of the post. Just as Mal was wondering why this damn fool wasn't down in the vault with everyone else, the man cried, "Take me with you!"

"Get in the vault with the others." Mal then turned his back on the man.

"I can't stay here! Please!"

Refusing to turn to look at the man, Mal said, "It's too many. Drive, Zoë."

And then he saw it.

First, truly, he heard it. The whine of the engine was much louder than any ship had a right to be, and that alone spoke to Reavers. They didn't concern themselves overmuch with radiation shielding or any other niceties, on account of they made their ships go slower.

No one knew where Reavers came from. Legend had it that they went out to the edge of the system, found a whole lotta nothing, then got all tweaked. Except not so much tweaked the way, say, River was tweaked, but tweaked in that they didn't care for nobody or nothing. Their ships were hodgepodges of dozens of types thrown together with little care for efficiency and less for aesthetics. Mal had seen one that had skinned corpses mounted on the hull, a sight

Mal knew he would take to his grave, right alongside the installation of a catalyzer.

The one that buzzed the rooftops of Lilac was about the size of *Serenity,* and was thankfully free of corpses. It looked like three different classes of ship welded together by a blind man, belching smoke from its engine, and painted with all manner of symbols Mal had no desire to decipher.

"Please!" The man sounded truly desperate now.

His jaw set, Mal looked at Zoë and said, "Drive!"

Zoë said nothing, but she didn't need to. It was her you're-the-captain-and-I'll-do-what-you-ask-but-I-don't-have-to-gorram-like-it face.

But they had no choice. Mule only sat four. A fifth body'd drag the thing, and they couldn't afford to lose any speed.

Course, by that logic they should dump their earnings. And, if it came to that, Mal'd consider it, but he wasn't in a position to go throwing money away just yet.

Besides, if that damn fool had gone to the vault like he was told . . .

Mal turned around, just as the man was jumped by four Reavers. As the mule pulled off, Mal couldn't make out any specifics, nor did he have any interest in doing so. The skin piercings, the clothes made of human epidermis, that was enough to identify them.

Unholstering his gun, Mal pointed it and fired two shots into the man's chest.

It was the kindest thing he could do for him now.

Even while that was happening, two more Reaver

ships—the one Mal saw a minute ago and an even bigger one—were hovering over the church. Cable lines fell to the ground, and Reavers went sliding down them.

Poor bastards don't stand a lick of a chance. Mal had to hope that at least the people in the vault would be safe. *Assuming the Reavers get bored and leave before the air runs out.*

As they left the town's outer border, a skiff shot out from behind one of the buildings, making a beeline for the mule. Jayne immediately fired a mess of shots at it, and it veered off. Their return fire was nothing to write home about.

"How come they ain't blowin' us out of the air?" Jayne asked.

"They wanna run us down," Mal said grimly. "The up-close kill."

In a tiny voice, River added, "They want us alive when they eat us."

A bullet went flying past Mal's head. *Which was why I shot that man. Could at least deny the Reavers one live meal.* Mal fired back.

Jayne gave Mal a smile that was wholly devoid of humor. "Boy, sure would be nice if we had some *grenades,* don'tcha think?"

Mal fired some more shots, refusing to dignify that with a response.

"Wash, baby, can you hear me?" That was Zoë, talking into the intercom.

The pilot's voice filtered through the speakers and the wind-whipping air. *"We're moments from air. You got somebody behind you?"*

"Reavers." Zoë managed to get a lot of meaning into one two-syllable word.

Wash muttered something in Chinese that Mal couldn't make out, but which he felt comfortable assuming was not fit for polite company.

Zoë looked back at the skiff, which was getting closer again. "We're not gonna reach you in time."

"Just keep moving, honey," Wash said. *"We're coming to you."*

Mal fired and nodded, grateful for Wash's good sense. *Serenity* cutting the distance improved their chances of actually making it to *Serenity* before they became Reaver lunch.

Jayne fired some more shots, then his gun clicked empty. He went for the ammo container—

—just as an arrow shot out from the skiff and shut it. Jayne tried to pry the case open.

Mal was about to tell Jayne not to leave himself open like that, but before he could say anything, a Reaver harpoon impaled Jayne right in the leg. The blade shot out the other side, the curved blade snapping up and bracing against the back of Jayne's thigh.

Not a second later, Jayne was flying through the air toward the skiff. If Mal hadn't already been prepared to warn Jayne, there wouldn't have been time, but with that, he was able to grab Jayne's arm.

"Grab on!" Mal cried.

Jayne, not being as stupid as he often was, caught on and grabbed the back of the mule, which was a steadier anchor than Mal's own unsecured self. Then he shouted, "I won't get et! You shoot me if they take me!"

Mal took aim with his gun.

His eyes wide, Jayne cried, "Well, don't shoot me *first!*"

However, Mal was not aiming at Jayne, much as it might've tickled him under other circumstances to make Jayne think so. He was, in fact, aiming for the harpoon line, which he finally got on the third shot.

Jayne's legs, which had been up above his head and behind him, fell without their tether and started dragging on the ground. Mal quickly grabbed his massive arms and helped him into the mule. They couldn't afford *any* kind of drag.

"Ruttin' pigs," Jayne was muttering as he clambered into the mule. "Where's—"

Before he could finish his question, River was holding out his gun.

Grinning, Jayne grabbed it and started firing.

Wash's voice returned over the intercom. *"Get some distance on 'em. You come to the flats, I want you to swing round. Gonna try a barn swallow. Simon, open her up!"*

Mal assumed that that last instruction was to the good doctor to open the cargo door. Mal had seen a "barn swallow" once before. Zoë was going to swing around and fly the mule in the same direction as *Serenity* and ahead of it. But *Serenity* would be going a mite faster, and would literally swallow up the mule. Once inside the cargo bay, Zoë would just have to speed the mule up to *Serenity*'s speed, which would put it at rest.

At least, that was how it was supposed to work.

When Mal saw it done, the pilot at the helm of the ship being swallowed was almost as good as Wash. Zoë had lots of fine qualities that made her the most valuable person in Mal's life, but she was only an average pilot.

Looking down at Jayne's impaled leg, he sighed. *We ain't exactly flush with alternatives.*

When they reached the flats, Zoë veered at some rocks, buzzing them closely enough to loosen them and send them flying into the Reavers. The skiff was forced to veer behind a rise, giving the mule a whole lotta extra room to make the U-turn they'd need in order to make Wash's magic trick work.

All right, maybe she's an above-average pilot . . .

Wash was making reassuring noises to his wife, which Mal appreciated, and kinda hoped for some directed at him. *"Okay, baby, we've talked this through."*

"Talkin' ain't doin'." That was Zoë, ever the pragmatist.

Then she threw the wheel, turning the mule around. Mal gripped the sides to keep from falling off. Jayne did likewise. To his confusion, River didn't hang onto anything, but stayed stock still.

Now, of course, they were heading right *for* the skiff.

C'mon, Wash. . . .

Then he heard another engine, but this the familiar—and properly shielded—whine of *Serenity. That's my girl. . . .*

Wash yelled, *"Don't slow down!"*

Wind whipped Mal's hair in all directions now as

Serenity's displacement made the air currents crazier than River.

And then, suddenly, Mal found himself within the confines of the cargo deck, flying straight past a stunned-looking Simon Tam at the door controls.

Just when Mal was ready to relax, a bone-jarring impact threw him straight from the mule, sending him flying to the deck.

It took him a moment to get his bearings, only to see that the mule had backed right into the large staircase that led to the catwalk. *Okay, only a* little *above average. At least the mule's more or less intact.*

So why do I smell smoke?

Rolling over on the deck, Mal saw flaming wreckage in the front of the cargo deck, followed a second later by CO_2 jetting out from the floor to smother the flame. *Must've been a piece of the Reaver skiff crashing into* Serenity. *Gorram Reavers . . .*

Mal climbed slowly to his feet, his head swimming more than a little. Zoë and River were still in the skiff. Jayne had also been thrown, and he was lying on the deck, grinning like an idiot. Simon was running over to the mule. "River?"

His sister popped her head out from inside the mule. She looked unhappy. "I swallowed a bug."

Kaylee came running in, then, and made a beeline for Simon. "Are you okay?"

Mal couldn't believe it. "Is *he* okay?"

However, before he could explain to Kaylee that her concern might've been better placed with the people who actually almost became Reaver lunchmeat as opposed to them that stayed behind and performed the strenuous tasks of pushing the "door open" button and pulling the fire extinguisher lever, a body popped out from the burned wreckage and lunged for Mal, his teeth bared.

Not just Mal, but Zoë and Jayne all unloaded their weapons into the Reaver.

He took some time to die. Far longer than any sane man would—but then, Reavers were no sane men. But eventually, the creature's body fell onto the singed skiff top.

This has been quite a day.

The cargo deck was silent for a moment, until Wash's voice came over the speakers. *"We all here? What's going on? Hello?"*

Zoë went over to the intercom and tapped the button with her gun. "No casualties. Anybody following?"

"Nice flying, baby, and that's a negative. Clean getaway—out of atmo in six minutes."

That was both a comfort and a burden to Mal. The former because the last time they'd come up against Reavers, they barely made it off the planet in one piece. The latter because the likeliest reason for the lack of pursuit was that the Reavers had plenty to keep them busy on Lilac.

He walked over to join Zoë at the intercom. "Set course for Beaumonde." Then he looked at Zoë. "First thing, I want this bod—"

The instruction was interrupted by the collision of Simon Tam's fist with Mal's jaw, which sent him stumbling.

In Chinese, Mal asked, "You wanna bullet? You wanna bullet right in your *throat?*"

Simon was shaking his hand in pain, which gave Mal a certain glee. "You stupid, selfish son of a whore!"

"I'm a hair's breadth from riddling you with holes, Doctor," Mal said in a low voice.

" 'One simple job.' " Simon threw Mal's words back in his face. " 'She'll be fine!' "

"She *is* fine. Except for bein' still crazy, she's the picture of health."

Before Simon could be stupid some more, Zoë put in, "Wasn't for River, we'd probably be left there. She felt 'em coming."

However, the doctor didn't seem interested in such minutiae. "Never again. You understand me?"

For someone so full of book learning, Dr. Tam could get a mite dense when the spirit moved him. "Seems I remember a talk about you giving orders on my boat."

"Well sleep easy, 'cause we're *off* your boat." Simon sounded as angry as Mal had ever heard him. In fact, thinking on it, Mal had *never* heard the child get angry before. "Just as soon as River gets her share of the bounty."

Kaylee looked like someone had killed her favorite hamster. "Well, let's not do anything hasty."

Mal, however, loved the idea. "No, shiny. I'm sick'a carrying tourists anyhow. We'll be on Beaumonde in ten hours' time, you can pick up your earnings and be on your merry. Meantime, you do your job." He pointed at Jayne and his harpoon wound. "Patch up my crew."

"He didn't lie down."

That was River. Mal, and everyone else, looked over at her. She was staring at the Reaver's corpse.

"They never lie down."

Mal found he couldn't say anything in response to that.

THE ACADEMY

Dr. Philbert Mathias was not having a good life.

Oh, it had been going fine. Top position at a government institute, working with cutting-edge science, expanding the boundaries of knowledge and possibility. It was work that every reputable scientist dreamed about.

Then it all went straight to hell.

Over the past eight months, Mathias had lost a quarter of his body weight, had acquired several dozen fresh gray hairs, and his superiors had made it clear that his continued employment was nowhere near a sure thing.

Then, on top of everything else, security informed him that someone was in the records room without authorization.

Accompanied by Sookdeo and Balbuena, two of the security guards, as well as Indira, the intern who had reported the intruder to security, Mathias stormed into the records room, intending to give the intruder a piece of his mind. The abused always kicked downward, and Mathias had been abused sufficiently that he was definitely in the mood to kick.

What he saw when he entered the long, spare room was a nondescript, dark-skinned man wearing wire-rimmed glasses and a suit that looked like it was almost a uniform, but for its lack of insignia. The man was viewing one of the holorecords.

To Mathias's irritation, the frozen image on the display was that of Dr. Simon Tam and his sister River making their way out of the complex. Or, as Mathias had come to think of it, the day his career ended.

Now *really* ready to do some kicking, Mathias bellowed, *"Excuse* me! No one is allowed in the records room without my express permission."

The stranger smiled. "Enter the doctor. Forgive me. I prefer to see the event alone, without bias."

Mathias would've been happy for no one ever to see that particular "event" again. "I need to see your clearance."

Nodding, the stranger said, "You're right to insist. I know you've had security issues here."

Mathias winced. *That was an unnecessary blow.*

The stranger placed his hand on one of the screens on the wall, and that screen then lit up with the record of who he was.

Realizing that no kicking would be going on today—at least not by Mathias himself—the doctor modified his tone to one of respect. "Apologies. An operative of parliament will, of course, have full co-operation." He glanced again at the screen, hoping for something to call him, but found nothing. "I'm not sure what— I see no listing of rank or name."

"I have neither. Like this facility, I don't exist. The parliament calls me in when—" The operative smiled. "—when they wish they didn't have to." The smile fell. "Let's talk about the Tams."

Mathias had figured that was inevitable, given what the operative was viewing. "I assume you've scanned the status logs."

"River was your greatest success. A prodigy, a phenomenon. Until her brother walked in eight months ago and took her from you."

In what he knew was a futile attempt to ameliorate the situation, Mathias said, "It's not quite so simple."

To Mathias's surprise, the operative said, "I'm very aware of that."

Encouraged by that statement, Mathias went on. "He came in with full creds. He beat the ap-scan, the retinal—there was no way I could—"

"No, no, of course. The boy spent his fortune developing the contacts to infiltrate this place."

Good, they're blaming Tam, not me. "Gave up a brilliant future in medicine as well, you've probably read. Turned his back on his whole life. Madness."

Shaking his head, the operative said, "Madness? No. Something a good deal more dangerous. Have you looked at this scan carefully?" He pointed to the frozen image of the Tam siblings on the display. "At his face?"

Mathias was at a loss, and just shrugged helplessly.

"It's *love,* in point of fact. He loved his sister, and he knew she was in pain. So he took her somewhere safe."

"Why are you here?" Mathias asked the question out of sheer desperation.

"I'm here because the situation is even less simple than you think. Do you know what your sin is, Doctor?"

Mathias didn't like the way this was going. "I—I would be very careful about what you—"

"It's pride."

At the touch of a control, the display changed to an image of Mathias talking with Simon when the former thought the latter was an inspector. Mathias was speaking: *"Key members of parliament have personally observed this subject. I was told their suppor—"*

The operative stopped the display again, Mathias's mouth frozen open, making him look foolish.

"Key members of parliament." The operative felt the need to repeat Mathias's words for some reason. "Key. The minds behind every diplomatic, military, and covert operation in the Alliance, and you put them in a room with a *psychic*."

This was what he was concerned with? Mathias couldn't believe it. "She was—she read cards, nothing more."

"It's come to our attention that River became much more unstable, more—disturbed after you showed her off to parliament."

Mathias's brain worked furiously. He hadn't noticed any particular correlation; thinking back, there may have been some coincidental timing, but River had been growing more unstable generally. He doubted parliament had anything to do with it.

Moving in far closer to Mathias than the doctor was comfortable with, the operative asked, "Did she see something very terrible in those cards?"

Quickly, Mathias said, "If there was some—classified information that she— Well, she never spoke of it. *I* don't know what it is."

"Nor do I. And, judging by her deteriorating mental state, I'd say we're both better off. Secrets are not my concern. *Keeping* them is."

"Whatever—secrets she might have accidentally gleaned—it's probable she doesn't even know she knows them. That they're buried beneath layers of psychosis." Mathias knew he was grasping at straws, but he was starting to have a very good idea how this conversation was going to end, and he didn't like it at all.

"But they *are* in her. Her mind is unquiet. It is the will of the parliament that I kill her. And the brother. Because of *your* sin." The operative moved toward a briefcase that was sitting near the display. "You know, in certain older civilized cultures, when men failed as entirely as you have, they would throw themselves on their swords."

Trying desperately to make a joke of it, Mathias said, "Well, unfortunately, I forgot to bring a sword to—"

With a crisp metallic sliding sound, the operative pulled a sword out of his briefcase. Mathias had never even *seen* a sword in person before. He knew some lunatics on the outer planets still used them, but to see one on a central planet . . .

"The parliament," the operative said as he held his sword in a manner that truly frightened Mathias, "has no further interest in psychics. They represent a threat to the harmony and stability of our Alliance."

Trying to maintain the dignity of his position, Mathias futilely said, "I would put that down right now if I were you."

"Would you be killed in your sleep, like an ailing pet? Whatever your failings, I believe you deserve better than that."

Mathias quickly shot Balbuena and Sookdeo a look. They both moved to stop the operative.

Moving faster than Mathias had ever seen a human being move, the operative sliced Balbuena's throat, then thrust at Sookdeo as the latter was unholstering his gun. The sword pinned Sookdeo's hand.

Deciding that discretion was the better part of getting the hell out of there, Mathias ran for the door, but the operative was on him in a flash, slamming him against the wall with an impact that Mathias felt all the way from his teeth to his toes.

Suddenly, a burst of pain shot through Mathias as the operative's hand slammed into the side of his spine.

Then he felt nothing at all.

Mathias blinked. From the neck down, he was completely immobile. He had no sensation, had no mental link to any of his limbs. *What did he do to me?*

The operative then dropped to one knee and held the bloody blade of his sword out to one side, hilt to the floor, and point up toward Mathias.

Although he couldn't feel his feet, Mathias did have the sensation of falling forward. *Oh, God, no . . .*

To Indira, the operative said, "Young miss, I'll need all the logs on behavioral modification triggers. We'll have to reach out to River Tam and help her come back to us. No matter how far out Simon has taken her, we can—"

Philbert Mathias didn't actually feel the blade slice into his chest and come out the other side as he fell on the blade. There was a mild sensation as if someone was pushing against his ribcage, but that was it.

The operative's face was now close to Mathias's. The doctor could feel his thoughts start to grow fuzzy and indistinct as the operative whispered to him. "This is a good death. There's no shame in this, in a *man's* death. A man who's done fine works. We're making a better world. All of them, better worlds."

Mathias had no idea what the operative was talking about. But then, he was having trouble focusing. His vision was growing fuzzy as well, as if the room had suddenly started to melt. . . .

"Young miss, I need you to get to work now. I think I may have a long way to travel."

Mathias knew the voice, but couldn't remember who it was. Or who he was talking to. Or where he was.

Or his name.

The last thing he heard before he forgot everything was: "Where are you hiding, little girl?"

As he walked through the foredeck hall toward his cabin, Mal asked Zoë, "You think I did wrong?"

"No," Zoë said, "I think things'll glide a deal smoother for us without River and Simon on board. But how long do you think *they'll* last?"

Mal knew the answer to that was, "Five, maybe six seconds," but refused to say it. He and Zoë both knew that, but it wasn't the point. "Doc made his call. They's as babes in a basket when we took 'em in. We sheltered 'em plenty. Man has to cut loose, learn to stand on his own."

As they arrived at the door to Mal's bunk, Zoë asked, "Like that man back in town?"

That brought Mal up short. "I had to shoot him. What the Reavers woulda done to him before they killed him—"

"I know," Zoë said, "that was a piece'a mercy. But before that, him begging us to bring him along."

Testily, because Zoë knew damn well what he was gonna say and why he was saying it, he said, "We couldn't take the weight. Woulda slowed us down."

"You know that for certain."

"Mule won't run with five. I shoulda dumped the girl? Or you? Or Jayne?" He considered. "Well, Jayne . . ."

Zoë, however, wasn't even in the mood for dark humor. "Coulda tossed the payload."

"And go to Fanty and Mingo with air in our mitts, tell 'em, 'Here's your share'? They'd set the dogs on us in the space of a twitch, and there we are back in mortal peril. We get a job, we gotta make good."

"Sir, I don't disagree on any particular point, it's just—" She hesitated. "In the time of war, we woulda never left a man stranded."

Mal opened the door to his bunk. "Maybe that's why we lost."

With that, he climbed down the ladder to his quarters. He'd had enough backchat for one hour.

Once he was down in his cabin, Mal took off his holster and tossed it to the floor, uncaring as to where it might land. There were assorted bits of crap on his bed, which he tossed onto the floor, not caring where they landed, neither.

However, one picture got his attention. A snapshot-movie, it started to play when it hit the deck. The still image was of a beautiful woman staring at the capture while standing in front of a shuttle that was elaborately decorated.

That same shuttle was sitting in one of *Serenity*'s bays, but it wasn't decorated no more, and the woman in the capture wasn't around no more, either.

Inara.

When it started moving, Inara said, *"Kaylee, are you ever gonna put that capture down?"*

Then Mal heard Kaylee's voice as he picked the snap up. *"We gotta have records of everything. A bona fide Companion entertained clients on this very ship! In this very bed!"* The picture panned over to the bed, which River was bending over and sniffing curiously, an image that, even in his mood, got a brief smile out of Mal. Inara was now packing. Kaylee was still carrying on: *"For one sweet second, we was almost classy."*

Inara looked back at the capture. *"You promised to help me pack."*

"Honest, Inara, why do you have to leave?"

Then the movie stopped, and the image reset to the first shot of Inara.

Mal dropped the snap to the floor.

Inara had come on board when Mal advertised for someone to rent one of the shuttles. They rarely needed more than one at a time, and the extra coin would come in handy. He'd gotten a few offers—a prospector couple, a holosculptor on the lookout for new subjects—but Mal had gone for Inara. Much as he hated what she did for a living, he had to admit that society viewed Companions as a sign of respectability. In his line of work, Mal could not afford to miss a chance to fool folk into thinking him respectable.

Inara was more than a nice curtain to put over the window, though. She had beauty, true, and elegance and style and compassion and intelligence and all the other things Companions were supposed to have. But Inara went way beyond that.

In the time she'd been on board, Inara became more than just the person who rented the shuttle. She'd become friends with everyone on the boat—excepting Jayne, of course, but including Shepherd Book, a notion that always struck Mal wrong. More to the point, she'd become family.

Kinda like the way Simon and River did.

The day Inara announced she was departing was a day Mal wouldn't soon forget, for all he'd wish himself able to. They'd just finished a job for a friend of Inara's who ran a whorehouse on a distant moon. Shunned by the Companion Guild, they had no one to turn to when a rich gent name of Ranse Burgess knocked up one of the whores and got it in his head to steal the child. Mal had spent the night prior to the showdown with Inara's friend, a former Companion named Nandi. Mal still had mixed feelings about that night, in particular thanks to Nandi getting herself shot and killed during that showdown.

Afterward, he and Inara talked a spell about any number of things, most relating to Nandi. Then she said, "I learned something from Nandi—not just from what happened, but from *her.* The family she made, the strength of her love for them, it's what kept them together. When you live with that kind of strength, you're tied to it—you can't break away, and you never want to."

Then she looked him square in the eye and spoke in that voice of hers that sounded like honey on bread: "There's something— There's something I should've done a long while ago—and I'm sorry for both of us that it took me this long. I'm leaving."

That, more than anything, reminded Mal of one

thing Inara *didn't* say in her pretty little speech about families: Eventually, they broke apart. Every time, without fail. That was the way of the 'verse, and there was nothing Mal could do about it.

So let the doc follow her and the shepherd out the airlock. It's about time we got back to basics anyhow. Go back to just takin' jobs, not worryin' about feds and bounty hunters and all that rainin' down on our pretty little heads.

The lack of a good medic was surely a drawback, but Mal did fine for six years on this boat without one, and a whole passel of what he needed medics for were taken in the line of keeping the feds away from the Tams.

Mal lay down on his bunk and stared at the ceiling a good long while.

— —

Standing on the cargo deck, Kaylee stole a glance up the stairs, toward where the infirmary was. Jayne had just returned from there, having his leg tended to by Simon. *Soon, he won't be doin' that no more,* she thought with a fair amount of wistfulness.

Kaylee had grown to really like Simon over the months. *Hell, it ain't just like.* Simon was good and strong and smart—and cute, dammit, he was cuter than anything. And the captain done went and drove him off, just like he drove off near everyone else.

Excepting Jayne of course. *It's just the nice folks he can't keep around.*

While Kaylee grabbed the controls for the deck doors, Jayne was hauling the Reaver corpse from its resting place to the middle of the deck. The notion was to open the inner door, dump the body into the crawlspace between the two sets of doors, close the inner door, depressurize the crawlspace, then open the outer door and let the body fly off into the black for a more proper burial than any Reaver really deserved.

"I do not get it. How's a guy get so wrong?"

At Jayne's words, Kaylee looked over at him and the corpse he was carrying. She pressed the button that opened the inner door.

Jayne went on: "Ain't logical. Cuttin' on his own face, rapin' and murdering—I mean, I'll kill a man in a fair fight. Or if I think he's gonna *start* a fair fight. Or if he bothers me. Or if there's a woman. Or I'm gettin' paid." He grinned. "Mostly only when I'm gettin' paid. But these Reavers—last ten years, they just show up like the bogeyman from stories. Eating people alive? Where does that get fun?"

As Jayne dropped the body into the crawlspace, Kaylee said, "Shepherd Book said they was men that reached the edge of space, saw a vasty nothingness, and just went bibbledy over it."

"Well, I been to the edge."

Kaylee managed to keep a straight face as she closed the inner door and started the depressurizing, but it wasn't easy.

Jayne shrugged. "Just looked like more space."

"I don't know. People get awful lonely in the black. Like to get addlepated ourselves, we stay on this boat much longer. Captain'll drive us all off, one by one."

Even as Kaylee spoke the words, she wished she could take them back. Of all the people on *Serenity*, Jayne was about the last one she should've been baring her soul to. All he'd do was make fun. Heck, all he'd done since Simon first came on board back on Persephone was make fun.

Sure enough, first thing he said was, "You're just in a whinge 'cause that prissy doc is finally disembarking. Me, I says good riddance."

Kaylee thought that was a particularly dim thing to say about someone who just fixed up his leg all nice, but she didn't want to say anything else that'd get her teased.

Jayne then added, "He never belonged here, and his sister's no saner than one of them Reavers."

That, Kaylee was willing to respond to. "That ain't even so! River's a dear heart and a boon to this crew. You just don't like her 'cause she can read your mind and everything you think is mean."

Jayne shrugged. "Well, there is that."

"Her and Simon could have a place here. Now they're leaving us. Just like Shepherd Book." Again, Kaylee looked up the stairs, this time toward one of the shuttles. "Just like Inara . . ."

COMPANION TRAINING HOUSE

Standing at the railing of a veranda overlooking the mountains, Inara imagined that this was what happiness felt like.

She had come to this training house on a border moon in order to teach prospective Companions in the ways of their guild. With the Alliance's borders constantly expanding, the need for their services would only increase in the outer worlds. Inara agreed with the guild's notion that proper training was better for all concerned than simply ignoring anyone who came out this far.

If this guild had been this enlightened a few years ago, Nandi might still be in *the guild—and still alive.*

Inara's own time spent on *Serenity* made her the perfect teacher for these young trainees. While she could train them in calligraphy and bowmanship and all the various methods of pleasure, she brought them something more important: experience. So much of Companion training was by guild members who were horribly sheltered. Inara was able to provide a perspective that she herself never got when she was training. Indeed, the hidebound nature of the higher-ups in the guild had a lot to do with why she sought out a ship to fly free on.

But the fact that the guild seemed to be learning from their mistakes made her decision to leave *Serenity* that much easier.

And it was easier.

Inara figured if she told herself that enough times, she might actually start to consider believing it.

Not that there weren't plenty of new mistakes to be made, if the children under her care were any indication.

Sheydra, an older woman who served as the superintendent of the training house, was preparing tea for both of them. She walked up to Inara and handed her a ceramic cup. "They love you, the girls. They've learned more from you these last months than the rest of us could show them in two years."

Inara took the cup, the heat of the tea warming her hands, the lovely scent of oolong tickling her nostrils. "They're very sweet." Then, deciding that it was best to be honest with Sheydra, she added, "But they're not Companions."

Wryly, Sheydra asked, "You've no hope for them? Junk the lot, start anew?"

"On Sihnon, we started training at twelve. Years of discipline and preparation before the physical act of pleasure was even mentioned. Most of these girls . . ."

"They're all of good family, the highest academic standards." Sheydra spoke as if that meant something.

Inara thought a moment. "Control was the first lesson. And the last. And these worlds are *not* like the central planets. There is barbarism dressed up in the most civil weeds. Men of the highest rank who don't know the difference between a Companion and a common whore. It's unsafe."

Unbidden, Inara's mind went to Atherton Wing, whom she had always thought a good man, but who turned out to be as coarse and brutal in his own way as Jayne Cobb, and Jayne at least had the indecency to be up front about it. Not to mention the casual brutality of the likes of Adlai Niska, Ranse Burgess, Magistrate Higgins . . .

"All the more reason the girls look to you," Sheydra said. "You came out here alone, before the Alliance ever thought to establish a House this remote. You've seen so much. You're a figure of great romance to them."

Rolling her eyes, Inara said, "Great romance has nothing to do with being a Companion, Sheydra. You should know better."

Sheydra's eyes twinkled. "I'm not the one who had a torrid affair with a pirate."

Inara almost lost her grip on the teacup. "A who? With a what?"

Smiling, Sheydra said, "It's the talk of the House. The girls all trade stories in the dorms at night."

"I didn't—" Inara was appalled, embarrassed, and disgusted all at the same time. "—*have* a pirate."

Thoughtfully sipping her tea, Sheydra said, "In one of the stories, you make love in a burning temple. I think that's my favorite."

Unable to believe what she was hearing, Inara sat

down. "This is unbearable. Captain Reynolds is no pirate, he's a petty thief. And he never laid a finger on me." *And someday, I may actually figure out how I feel about that.* She refused to say that to Sheydra, though, as it would only make things worse. "All he ever did was rent me a shuttle and be very annoying." In Chinese, she muttered, "A switch to those girls' backsides is just good enough . . ."

Sheydra shook her head. "A year on his shuttle, and he never laid a finger on you? No wonder you left."

"I left because—" Shifting so her back was to Sheydra, Inara petulantly said, "Go away. We're no longer friends. You're a stranger to me now."

Laughing, Sheydra said, "I do love to watch you boil. Don't worry, the stories will fade. And your Captain Reynolds has probably gotten himself blown up by this time."

Inara thought about Atherton, she thought about that awful bounty hunter named Early, she thought about Niska torturing Mal and cutting off his ear, she thought about Patience ambushing Mal and Zoë on Whitefall, she thought about Saffron or Bridgit or Yolanda or whatever her name was and her attempts to con the crew, and she thought about all the other people Mal had managed to annoy just in the year that she'd been on *Serenity,* and decided that Sheydra's prediction was not unfounded.

"Yes," she said with a sigh, "that would be just like him."

Just like him to go and die before I had the chance to tell him anything.

A small voice in Inara's head said: *You had your chance to tell him everything, and you ran away from the ship instead. That's hardly Mal's fault.*

Inara sipped her tea and told the small voice to go jump in a lake.

BEAUMONDE

River watched the people go by at the port where *Serenity* had landed on Beaumonde. From the way everyone was talking, this was where Simon and River would leave *Serenity*. This made River both happy and sad.

Sad because *Serenity* was her first home. The Tam estate was a place where she lived, but it was never home. When she read the literature about the academy, she thought that there, surrounded by other intelligent children and teachers who were used to intelligent children—as opposed to the hopeless adults like Professor Rao who tried and failed to impart knowledge to her at school—she might find a place. But that proved a false hope.

Happy because she knew that her continued presence on *Serenity* would only lead to the crew getting hurt. And River didn't want to see Kaylee or Zoë or Wash or Captain Reynolds get hurt. She didn't mind seeing Jayne get hurt, but that was only because Jayne betrayed them at Ariel and tried to turn them in to the feds, and only failed because the feds turned on him and didn't give him his reward.

Besides, it didn't matter how many times Jayne got hurt. He would continue to survive. On Earth-That-Was, or so she'd read, the only creatures who were able to survive great cataclysms were cockroaches. Jayne was like a cockroach in that sense. Most senses, if it came right down to it.

People of almost every shape and size walked by the open cargo ramp to *Serenity*. The only type of people missing were people like River's parents. There were no wealthy people on Beaumonde. But there were plenty of others. A slovenly man walked up to an elegant-looking woman and, in Chinese, offered his services. She refused in the same language. For fun, River translated what they said into English, Italian, Latin, Greek, Esperanto, Japanese, Russian, and Tobrik. That last was a tongue that River herself made up when she was eleven. She was bored one day, and so decided to create an entire language. To make it a special challenge, she made the language not have the verb "to be." It was fine right up until she tried to translate *Hamlet*.

While River was people-watching, Kaylee was talking to Simon. It was because of Kaylee especially that River was glad to be leaving *Serenity*. Kaylee was River's closest friend besides Simon, and Kaylee and Simon were also in love with each other. The only reason they hadn't done anything about it was because her brother was too stupid to live.

River didn't want to see Kaylee hurt. So it was good that they were leaving.

"Don't talk to the barkers," Kaylee was saying,

"only to the captains. You look the captain in the eye, know who you're dealing with."

That, River found funny. When Simon signed on to *Serenity,* he had only talked to the barker, who happened to be Kaylee herself. River suspected that if Simon had followed that advice with regards to *Serenity,* Simon never would have chosen that ship.

Simon thumphered. "I wish there was—" He couldn't find the words.

Mal walked by then, studiously ignoring all three of them. Zoë and Wash were waiting for him on the concourse. The man who'd accosted the elegant woman looked at Zoë and said, still in Chinese, "Pretty lady, forget him and hire me!"

Zoë gave the man a look that, if looks could kill, would have decapitated him. Wash just said, "My wife is not pretty!" Zoë then transferred her death gaze to her husband.

Kaylee went on: "You shouldn't oughtta be so clean. It's a dead giveaway you don't belong, you always gotta be tidy."

River knew that Simon deliberately kept himself bathed and groomed the way he did because it was his way of holding on to his old life. Even though he was never happy in his old life, he insisted on it. It was another reason why her brother was too stupid to live.

"Don't pay anybody in advance," Kaylee added. "And don't ride in anything with a Capissen 38 engine, they fall right out of the sky."

"Kaylee."

River shot Simon a look. Her stupid brother managed to fit a lot of longing and pain into that one word.

Kaylee just gave him an equally longing and pained look back, then went to join Mal and the others.

Simon looked at her. "River, do you want to stay with them?"

"It's not safe."

Sighing, Simon said, "No, I fear it's not safe anymore."

He walked off. River rolled her eyes. *Definitely too stupid to live.* "For them," she said, but Simon didn't hear her.

--

Mal led the rest of his crew down the concourse toward the Maidenhead, the bar where the meet with Fanty and Mingo was to be taking place. CorVue screens were all over the place, and their big story was the familiar sight of Lilac. Unlike the town they'd entered only a short while ago, the place was now a smoking ruin. As Mal, Zoë, Wash, Kaylee, and Jayne walked, a new screen would come into view and earshot just as the one they passed was no longer useful to them. *That's the Alliance, always makin' sure we're nice and informed no matter where we're standin'.*

Mal also knew that each screen doubled as a surveillance camera.

The anchor's voice provided a handy distraction from Kaylee wailing on about Simon.

"Devastation and murder on the small border

*moon of Lilac just yester as a breakpack settlement is
ravaged by what some settlers say may have been
Reavers."*

Mal couldn't believe it. *May have been? What other
ruttin' thing could cause that? Rabid beagles?*

"I can't believe you just let Simon walk away like
that," Kaylee said, which was all she'd been saying
since they left *Serenity.*

The anchor continued: *"There is no way to confirm
that, however, as the only survivors were hidden away
and never saw a thing. Our cam is waving now and
here's the patch."*

"Any particular way you'd've preferred I let him
walk away?"

"That ain't funny, Cap'n."

"C'mon, Kaylee, it was a *little* funny."

Kaylee started to sulk, which was as sad a sight as
Mal ever saw.

The CorVue image switched to that of the very
guard from whom Mal had liberated the Alliance payroll. He was looking a sight more mussed than he had
been when Mal last laid eyes. *"Can you tell us what
you saw?"* the anchor's now-offscreen voice asked.

Sounding a lot more excitable, the guard said,
*"Well, someone started screaming 'Reavers!' We heard
noises and ships—I was in the trade station, and I—I
thought it was best to protect the—the people. So we
went into the vault. From my idea."*

Under other circumstances, Mal would've been a
mite peevish over another man taking credit for his
work, but anything that kept the notion that he was

ever even on Lilac out of folks' heads was something of which he heartily approved.

"So," the anchor said to the guard, *"you never actually saw any Reavers?"*

"No, but we heard—things. And we seen after, the bodies they didn't take. Whole families that were—" The guard visibly shivered. *"I'd say it was Reavers."*

"No Alliance government has ever officially confirmed the existence of Reavers." The guard sounded like an Alliance magistrate.

The guard snapped, *"Well, no Alliance government ever saw someone where their face got et! Reavers is just crazy people—and who all ever did what they did to the people in that church, I'd surely grade them crazy."*

Apparently wholly oblivious to the guard's righteous anger, the anchor said, *"You're our hero of the day! You've won a vacation for two on Boarshead Inn at Dennon Rocks! Who do you plan to bring along?"*

Looking away at someone off-screen, the guard, sounding about as disgusted as Mal felt, said, *"Can you turn that thing off now? Turn that rutting thing off."*

Unable to stand the look on Kaylee's face any longer, Mal said, "It's not my fault the doc's got no stomach for rim living."

"It is entirely and for all your fault! If you'd given Simon a moment, just a moment where he didn't think you were gonna throw them off or turn them in, he might've—"

"What? Swept you into his cleanly arms? Made

107

tidy love to you?" Mal refrained from pointing out that he'd given Simon plenty of such moments, not least when they went back and rescued them from hill folk on Jiangyin. However, Mal suspected that Kaylee wasn't of a mind to be told that right present.

Zoë, Wash, and Jayne all cracked smiles at Mal's words, but Kaylee fixed him with as fierce a look as she'd ever given him. "Don't you dare joke!"

They had reached the gun check for the Maidenhead. First Wash, then Zoë, then Jayne, then finally Mal each put their gun in a drawer and were given a claim chit in return. This process was supervised by the not-terribly-watchful eye of a bouncer who looked about as bored as Jayne would be at a poetry reading. On the CorVue, the anchor was carrying on about showing more footage of Lilac later on at an "age-appropriate hour."

Kaylee, who had no gun to check, was still ranting, making Mal nostalgic for the sulking. "You know how much I pined on Simon. And him fair sweet on me, I well believe, but he's so worried about being found out—"

Zoë, bless her, came to his rescue. "Captain didn't make 'em fugitives."

"But he coulda made 'em family, 'steada driving them off."

Mal winced at that, remembering Inara's words to him right before she told him she was leaving.

Kaylee wasn't finished. " 'Steada keeping Simon from seein' I was there, when I carried such a torch and we coulda— Goin' on a year now I ain't had nothin' twixt my nethers weren't run on batteries."

Mal felt queasy. "Oh, God, I can't know that!"

Grinning, Jayne raised his hand. "I could stand to hear a little more."

Amazingly, Kaylee didn't react to that, instead just glaring at Mal. "If you had a care for anybody's heart, you woulda—"

That was the straw that broke. "You knew he was gonna leave! We never been but a way station to those two. And how do you know what he feels? He's got River to worry on, but he still coulda shown you— If I truly wanted someone bad enough, wouldn't be a thing in the 'verse could stop me from going to her."

"Tell that to Inara."

Mal's mouth hung open. *Dammit, I done walked right into that one.*

Even if Mal had been able to form a response, Kaylee wouldn't have heard it, as she chose that as her exit line.

"Domestic troubles?"

Mal turned to see two identical twins. It was Fanty who had spoken.

Mingo then added, " 'Cause we don't wanna interrupt."

"A man should keep his house in order," Fanty added.

Mal looked at each. "Mingo. Fanty."

Mingo pointed at his brother. "*He's* Mingo."

Smirking, Mal said, "He's Fanty. You're Mingo."

"Gah!" Mingo looked angered, as he always did whenever he tried and failed to fool Mal. "How is it you always know?"

"Fanty's prettier." Truth be told, Mingo's voice was a mite higher than Fanty's. He could tell one from the other even over a bad wave. Pulling out a seat, Mal parked himself in it. "Feel to do some business?"

Mingo looked at Zoë, Wash, and Jayne. "Bit crowded, innit? As you see, we come unencumbered by thugs."

Mal snorted. "Which means at least four of the guys already in here are yours. All's one. I'll just keep Jayne with me."

"Sir," Zoë said, "are you sure you don't—?"

"Go." He had to let somebody go, and he preferred the idea of Jayne underfoot where he could step on him rather than roaming about without adult supervision. "Go get yourselves a nice romantic meal."

Smiling, Wash said, "Those are my two favorite words!" Zoë gave him her why-did-I-marry-you-again? look, to which Wash just said, "Honey? 'Meal'?"

Trying to sound reassuring, Mal said, "It's business. We're fine."

After giving Fanty and Mingo her don't-even-*think*-about-messing-with-my-captain look, Zoë let Wash lead her out of the Maidenhead.

Fanty tossed a few coins to one of the saloon girls, who started doing a fan dance. As Fanty, Mingo, and Jayne all sat down, Mal noted that the girl was dancing in a particular spot that blocked their table from the CorVue's camera. Fanty and Mingo could be the most annoying cusses this side of Persephone, but they weren't no fools.

Mal's foot nudged the duffel containing the twins' share of the job to Mingo's foot.

Mingo, however, didn't acknowledge it. "Quite a crew you've got."

"Yeah," Mal said, "they're a fine bunch of reubens."

"How you keep them on that crap boat is the subject of much musing 'tween me and Fanty."

Fanty added, "We go on and on."

"So I'm noticing. Is there a problem I don't know of? You got twenty-five percent of a sweet take kissing your foot, how come we're not dispersing?"

Smiling the kind of smile that made Mal want to check his pockets, Fanty said, "Our end is forty, precious."

His hand going to his sadly empty holster, Jayne said, "My muscular buttocks it's forty!"

Great, Mal thought, *now that image is gonna be in my head all the livelong day . . .*

"It is as of now," Mingo said. "Find anyone around going cheaper."

"Find anyone around going near a sorry lot like you in the *first* instance," Fanty said.

Jayne nudged Mal and indicated the entrance. Mal turned to see River entering. Mal shrugged and turned back to the twins. He needed to focus on their cheating selves, not crazy young'uns.

Fanty was still going on and on. "You're unpredictable, Mal, which is the single worst thing to be in this business. Mingo and me, we're greedy. Could set your watch by our greed. It wavers never. But you—you run when you oughtta fight, fight when

111

you oughtta deal. Makes a businessperson twitchy."

Mingo then picked it up. "Adding in the fact that your ship's older than the starting point of time and you can see you's charity cases to the likes of us."

A thought occurred to Mal that, in the hustling and bustling of the day's events, had slipped on by him till now. "Well, here's a foul thought: I conjured you two were incompetent. Sent us out not knowing there were Reavers about. Now I'm thinking you picked us out because you *did*."

Mingo shrugged. "That were a sign of faith, boy. And it doesn't affect our forty per. Danger is, after all, your business."

Jayne snarled. "Reavers ain't business, double dickless."

Mal stole a glance over at River for a moment. She was now standing under the CorVue screen, which was showing some manner of advertisement for Fruity Oaty Bars. The jingle would need to improve a fair piece before it got as good as inane, and the images looked like they came straight from River's own twitchy mind.

Naturally, River was captivated.

Then, suddenly, her face got all blank-like and she whispered the word, "Miranda."

What happened next happened very quickly.

Moving a damn sight faster than any sixteen-year-old girl had any business moving, she strode over to the nearest table, where two men were sharing a drink. Then they both shared being on the receiving end of two well-placed kicks from a girl that took them both out.

They weren't just any kicks. Them was kicks by

folks were trained to it. Aside from that bounty hunter fella named Early, Mal had never seen anyone kick like that in person.

River wasn't close to done. She kicked the two men's table into a card player at the next one, even as she swept a bottle off it behind her. That bottle hit a fella square on the nose, which was quite a feat, seeing as how the man was behind River.

"Whu-huh?" That was Jayne, who, like most of the bar, was taking notice of the little girl who'd just taken out four of the bar's patrons without even working up a sweat. Four more folk tried to gang up on her, and she took them as well, clocking the fourth one before the first one had a chance to hit the floor.

Two men came at her from either side—one brandishing a knife—doubtless secure in the notion that she couldn't take 'em both. River relieved them of that notion by doing a perfect split, thus ducking both attacks, then reached up over her head and grabbed the wrist of the knife guy and used his momentum to stab the other one.

"Hey, a tussle!" Jayne was always one for showcasing his keen grasp of the obvious.

"Jayne . . ." Mal said in warning.

As soon as River began her little spree, two things happened. The first was that the bouncer had come a-running with his shockrod, looking a damn sight less bored. It hadn't taken him long to get to her, but she'd made impressive use of the time. The second was that three men of considerable body weight moved to stand between River and the twins.

Without even a little effort, River relieved the bouncer of his shockrod and used it on him. Mal had been on the receiving end of a shockrod once—at a tavern on Boros where someone took umbrage to either Mal's brown coat, his attitude, or his sweet smile, he wasn't sure which—and he was not eager to relive the experience. He had lain twitching on the floor for the better part of an hour, and couldn't walk in a straight line for a week.

After finishing with the bouncer, who fell to the floor to commence his own hour of twitchiness, River then used the shockrod on Fanty and Mingo's three bodyguards.

Now Jayne's jaw had dropped open. "River?"

Fanty and Mingo looked a lot like Jayne did. Fanty asked, "You know that girl?"

Without equivocation, Mal said, "I really don't." River had done all manner of crazy since Mal defrosted her cryo chamber eight months back, but this was an entirely new breed. He picked up the duffel and practically shoved it into Mingo's hands. "Get out."

"Don't tell us what to do," Mingo said angrily, even as he and Fanty made a run for it.

Some managed to get out of the Maidenhead. Others weren't so lucky. River was simply *everywhere*. She kicked around a corner to kick a man she couldn't see right in the face.

Mal made a line for the gun holder. The bouncer, still twitching away, was in no position to stop him.

Jayne, meanwhile, made what Mal could've told

him was a major tactical blunder, had he bothered to ask: He grabbed her from behind.

"Gorrammit, girl, it's *me!*"

River's predictable response to that was to reach behind her, grab Jayne's crotch, and squeeze tight. The look on Jayne's face might have been funny in a different time and place. She then turned around, flat-heeled his nose with her palm, then doubled him over with a gut kick. While cracking Jayne's thick head on a table, she then kicked another fool in the face.

Somebody who had managed to sneak a gun past the bouncer—or was on Fanty and Mingo's payroll—pulled out his weapon even as Mal finally got the drawer open to get his.

River grabbed the man's arm and snapped his elbow with a sickening crunch. The man screamed in pain and shot himself in the gut, no small feat. Then she knocked the man's gun in the air, kicked someone else who hadn't learned the futility of a frontal assault, and then caught the gun just as Mal got his out of the drawer.

He pointed his weapon at her just as she pointed hers at him.

After surviving the war, torture, and living with Jayne Cobb, to wind up being shot in a bar on Beaumonde by a sixteen-year-old crazy girl would be downright embarrassing. And fairly in keeping, truth be told.

Then Mal heard a familiar voice call out some unfamiliar words. "Eta kooram nah smech!"

River dropped to the ground, fast asleep.

Mal turned toward the door to see Simon standing there. He had uttered that nonsense phrase, which seemed to have done what a bar full of the toughest folk on this world couldn't. Mal also noted that aside from Simon, he himself was the only person still in the bar standing.

Then he looked down at River again. She looked like a little angel, asleep like that—which served as a fine reminder as to why Mal no longer believed in angels.

He looked back at the doctor. "I think maybe we ought to leave."

Simon nodded.

THE OPERATIVE'S VESSEL

The operative could not remember the time before he became an operative of parliament. This was not due to any flaw, but rather to training: Those memories had been removed, deemed both irrelevant and detrimental to his ability to perform his function. He was as the limbs to the parliament's brain, carrying out their instructions.

To carry the analogy further, the information he had obtained from Dr. Mathias served as the central nervous system, directing the limbs' actions.

In order to locate River Tam, he needed to get a message to her, and he needed a delivery system that would have at least a chance of working. His solution, so brilliant because it was so mundane, was to use the one thing seen by more people than all else: advertisements. Ads were quite literally everywhere, and no matter where Simon may have taken River, it was unlikely that she would be able to escape the inundation of advertising.

Sooner or later, she would come across an ad for

Fruity Oaty Bars. And then the first phase would be complete.

Sure enough, she did—on Beaumonde in a disreputable establishment of the type that invariably came into being regardless of how hard the Alliance tried to stamp them out. Human nature was never an easy thing to change.

Standing on the bridge of his ship, the operative watched the feed from the Maidenhead. At one point, River looked right at the CorVue camera. Smiling, the operative said, "Hello again. Yes, it's me. I'm glad you've finally asked for me."

Ensign Carmelito said, "We got a pos on a retinal—man carrying her out is Malcolm Reynolds. Captains a *Firefly*-class transport ship, *Serenity*. Bound by law five times, smuggling, tariff dodge— not convicted." Carmelito shrugged. "Nothing here that would—"

"The ship. The name of the ship." The operative already knew of the connection between the Tams and Reynolds. A fed named Dobson had boarded Reynolds's ship and then both Dobson and the ship disappeared after Dobson called in. The fed had taken a second shot at the crew a few months ago and, again, failed. A bounty hunter named Jubal Early was last reported to be chasing down the Tams, and then disappeared without a trace. A simple salvage vessel shouldn't have been so safe a haven. But something about the name *Serenity* . . .

Softly to the computer in his spectacles, the operative said, "Crossref: Malcolm Reynolds, Serenity."

Text started to scroll on his lens. The operative smiled.

"Sir?" Carmelito asked, sounding confused.

"Serenity Valley. Bloodiest battle of the entire war." Some of the information came from the scrolling text, but he actually knew most of it already. He had only needed the prompt. "The Independents held the valley for seven weeks, two of them *after* their high command had surrendered. Sixty-eight percent casualty rate."

"Of course, sir," Carmelito said. "I just didn't—"

The text hit Reynolds's service record, and the operative said, "There." The scrolling stopped. The operative studied the text in front of his eyes and shook his head. "If the feds ever bothered to crossref justice files with war records. Yes, our Mr. Reynolds was a sergeant, 57th Overlanders. Volunteer. Fought at Serenity till the very last." Now it made sense—Dobson, Early, how the Tams had remained safe. "This man is an issue. This man hates us."

Carmelito had called up the rest of the records of the 57th and crossreffed. "First mate Zoë Washburne, formerly Corporal Zoë Alleyne, also in the 57th. Career army, looks like."

"She's followed him far." That kind of loyalty could only be inspired by the best leaders. The operative was starting to think that Tam had chosen his refuge quite well indeed. To his spectacles, he said, "Give me the crew, registered passengers." He sighed. "Our captain is a passionate man, no room for subtlety. He's bound to have some very obvious—"

Then he saw it. A licensed Companion named Inara Serra who had rented one of *Serenity*'s shuttles for a year, and who had recently ended that arrangement to teach at the new Companion Training House.

"—weakness," he finished with a smile.

For reasons that were obvious to everyone except Simon Tam, Mal chained River up in a storage locker back on *Serenity*. Dragging Jayne's sorry carcass back to the boat was a chore and a half, but Mal managed it, aided by Zoë and Wash, who met him partway, having heard about the ruckus while searching for romantic dining opportunities. Wash had taken *Serenity* away from Beaumonde and toward Haven as fast as possible, Mal not being keen on waiting for Fanty and Mingo to decide that they wanted the other fifteen percent, especially after a member of Mal's crew tore up their place. Mal wasn't particularly keen on *giving* them that fifteen percent, regardless of River's spree, so he got gone quick-like.

Aside from Wash, who was in the cockpit, Mal had asked everyone else to gather in the dining room—including Simon. Jayne was standing proximate to the doctor, giving him the hairy eyeball. Zoë and Kaylee sat at the table. Mal remained standing.

"May I see her?" Simon asked.

"She's still napping just now," Mal said. "And I believe you've got some storytelling to do."

Before that story could commence, Wash came in. "We're out of atmo, plotted for Haven. No one following as of yet."

Kaylee perked up at that. "Haven? We're gonna see Shepherd Book?"

Mal nodded. "We got to lay low. And I could fair use some spiritual guidance right about now." He glowered at Simon. "I am a lost lamb. What in *hell* happened back there?"

Grinning as he took a seat next to Zoë, Wash said, "Start with the part where Jayne gets knocked out by a ninety-pound girl. 'Cause I don't think that's *ever* getting old."

Jayne transferred his dirty look from Simon to Wash, who ignored it.

Zoë asked, "Do we know if anyone was killed?"

Thinking on that man who gut-shot himself after River broke his arm, Mal said, "It's likely. I know she meant to kill me 'fore the doc put her to sleep—" He looked back at Simon. "—which how exactly does that work anyhow?"

"Safeword." Simon took a breath. "The people who helped me break River out, they had intel that River— and the other subjects—were being embedded with behavioral conditioning. They taught me a safeword in case something happened."

Kaylee frowned. "Not sure I get it."

Seeming grateful to be talking to someone other than Mal, Simon told her, "A phrase that's encoded in her brain, that makes her fall asleep. If I speak the words, 'eta—' "

Jayne jumped back. "Well, don't *say* it!"

Giving Jayne her remind-me-why-I-haven't-killed-you-yet? look, Zoë said, "It only works on *her,* Jayne."

"Oh." Jayne straightened up. "Well, now I know that."

Mal was eager to return to an earlier part of Simon's tongue-wag. " 'In case something happened.' "

Simon looked confused. "What?"

"You feel to elaborate on what 'something' might be? I mean, they taught you that fancy safeword, they must've figured she was gonna, what—start uncontrollably crocheting?"

"They never said what—"

"And you never did ask." Mal grabbed Simon and threw him against the bulkhead. "Eight months! Eight months you had her on my boat, knowing full well she might go monkeyshit at the wrong word, and you never said a *thing.*"

Acting remarkably composed for a man Mal was ready to throttle to death, Simon said, "I brought her out here so they couldn't get to her, I don't even know how they—"

Mal didn't want to hear it. *"My* ship! My *crew!* You had a gorram time bomb living with us! What if she went off in the middle of dinner, or in bunk with Kaylee—did that give you a moment's pause?"

Simon's head turned toward Kaylee, looking stricken as all get-out, as Mal's words sunk in.

Weakly, Simon said, "I thought she was getting better."

"An' I thought they was gettin' *off!*" Everyone

looked at Jayne after he said those words. "Didn't we have a intricate plan how they was gonna be not here anymore?"

Kaylee said, "We couldn't leave 'em *now!*"

"No, now that she's a—killer woman we ought to be bringin' 'em tea and dumplings!" Jayne turned to Mal. "In earnest, Mal: Why'd you bring her back on?"

Mal let go of Simon, but said nothing, because in earnest, he had no idea why he'd taken them back. The smart play would've been to burn engine out of Beaumonde, with Simon and River eating wake.

Then he recollected Fanty's words: "You run when you oughtta fight, fight when you oughtta deal."

Am I doing that again?

Well, it wouldn't be the first time. Anyone with sense would've let Serenity Valley go. Anyone with sense would have run away rather than face Atherton Wing in a swordfight. Anyone with sense wouldn't have let Saffron back on his boat a second time. But Mal had always found sense to be highly overrated.

Again, Simon asked, "May I see her?"

Mal stepped aside and let him go.

After Simon departed for the storage locker, Jayne said, "She goes woolly again, we're gonna have to put a bullet in her."

"It's crossed my mind," Mal said quietly.

Wash raised his hand. "Can I make a suggestion that doesn't involve violence—or is this the wrong crowd?"

"Honey—" Zoë started, but Wash kept going.

"Fanty and Mingo might be coming hard down on

us, or the laws—or maybe nobody could be bunged about our little social brawl. We need to get our bearings. I think we need to talk to Mr. Universe."

Mal turned to Wash. "That may be the best idea I've heard all day." He let out a chuckle that was fair without mirth. "Which is a sad commentary on my day. Make it happen, Wash. Let's see Mr. Universe."

MR. UNIVERSE'S MOON

Hoban Washburne was second in his class in flight school. The guy who was first didn't achieve that due to any actual piloting skill—he in fact had none whatsoever—but because he hacked his way into the computers and made them do what he wanted. Every time he entered the simulator, it flew perfectly because he told it to days earlier. Every time he got into an actual ship, he had preprogrammed it to do on autopilot precisely what the lesson called for. Even when he did poorly—some of the exercises simply could *not* be preprogrammed and required actual skill to do right— he hacked into the computers that held the grades and changed them to perfection.

Wash had known him as an unhygienic young man named Manfred Asbach, but that name turned out to be a fake one he'd created just for flight school; he wanted to say he was a certified pilot, despite being unable to actually fly a ship.

The only name he would answer to was "Mr. Universe." In addition to the pilot's certification, he was also an ordained shepherd, a professional planet-diver, and a licensed prospector, though he could perform none of those tasks, either.

After a while, he grew tired of being in more than one place, and so hacked into the computers of a communications complex and had them inform the owner of the complex that the terraforming on the moon they were using was becoming undone, and that the atmo would be unbreathable inside a month. They pulled out quickly, and Mr. Universe pulled in, setting himself up with dozens of computers and the ability to penetrate almost any electronic device in the 'verse. His only company was a Love-Bot™ named Lenore. He'd had Lenore since flight school, truth be known.

Mr. Universe had remained off the Alliance's radar simply by never letting them know he existed. He had such a tremendous facility with computers that it was impossible for there to be any trace of him. Wash knew who he was only because Wash confronted him at graduation, refusing to believe that someone so inept could beat him out.

When Mr. Universe told him the truth, Wash had two choices. The first was to beat him up; the second to keep Mr. Universe's secret in exchange for occasionally making use of his services. The problem with the first option was that Wash was not a fighter. He couldn't even take Lenore. The latter option struck him as a better long-term benefit—besides, second in his class in flight school wasn't too bad, all things.

When they arrived at the moon—which scanners still read as having a poisoned atmo—Wash, Zoë, and Mal went down. Jayne and Kaylee had both refused to come. Jayne because, "That weirdo ain't right in the head," which was hilarious coming from Jayne; Kaylee because she always felt like she needed to bathe for several days after talking to Mr. Universe.

Zoë, in truth, felt like Kaylee did, but Mr. Universe was convinced that Zoë had the hots for him, so he was always more gregarious around her—because he took pity on her obsession, supposedly. Wash didn't rightly care, as long as he stayed gregarious, and Zoë could take it.

When they arrived in Mr. Universe's little love nest—consisting of about a thousand computers and two chairs, the second one for Lenore—they told them what happened on Beaumonde. Before Mal had even finished the story, Mr. Universe's hands were flying across several different keyboards at once, and soon one of the dozens of screens in front of him—all of which were showing something or other, none of which Wash wanted to know the details of—showed one of the camera feeds from the Maidenhead. Wash actually was grateful for that, as he hadn't gotten to see River in action. He especially enjoyed the part where she grabbed Jayne's privates, and wondered if Mr. Universe would consider making him a copy of just that part.

"Oh, this is good," Mr. Universe was muttering. "This is— She's beating up all the burly men and I'm having a catharsis, it's happening right now."

Wash winced. He'd seen Mr. Universe's catharses firsthand, and they usually required a fastwipe afterward.

"You guys always bring me the best violence. You think you're in a hot place?"

"That's what we're looking to learn," Wash said. "Is there any follow-up? A newswave?"

Mr. Universe giggled. "There is no 'news.' There's the truth of the signal, what I see, and there's the puppet theatre the parliament's jesters foist on the somnambulant public. Monkey taught to say the word 'monkey,' lead story on thirty-two planets. But the slum riots on Hera? Not a—"

Mal interrupted, which made Wash wince. Mal had known Mr. Universe long enough to know that he didn't like being interrupted in mid-rant. That alone told Wash how worried Mal was. "What about *this?*" He pointed at the image of River carving through the patrons of the Maidenhead. "Did this make the puppet theatre?"

"No, sir. And no lawforce flags, either. I hadda go into the security feed direct."

"You can do that?" Mal asked, even though he knew full well that he could. Wash suspected that Mal had realized his earlier *faux pas* and was covering by giving Mr. Universe a chance to show off.

"Can't stop the signal, Mal. Everything goes somewhere and I go everywhere. Security feeds are a traipse to access. And I wasn't the first one in, this has prints on it." The feed got to the part where River took out four people in succession with a shockrod. "Oh! Look at her go! Everyone is getting bruises and contusions. Contooooooooooooooooosions!"

Recognizing rightly that Mr. Universe would be

focused on contusions for a bit, Zoë turned to Mal. "So somebody else has been fed this. That doesn't like me too well."

Mr. Universe looked up at Zoë with pity. "Zoë, you sultry minx, stop falling in love with me. You're just gonna embarrass yourself." He tapped a bunch of keys, and then one of the monitors changed to a shot of this very space, but with Mr. Universe in a fancy tuxedo and Lenore in the same seat and position but wearing a wedding dress. Mr. Universe stepped on a cup, then tossed confetti and waved at the camera. "I have a commitment to my Love-Bot™. It was a very beautiful ceremony, Lenore wrote her own vows, I cried like a *baby*, a hungry, angry baby." The nearer screen got to the part where Mal and River had their standoff, until Simon said the magic word. River fell to the floor. "And she falls asleep. Which, she would be sleepy."

"Can you go back?" Mal asked. "See if anybody spoke with her 'fore she acted up, made any kind of contact with her?"

At Mr. Universe's command, the fight rewound to just before River started the melée by taking out two men with one kick. She was staring right at the screen now, and she whispered the word "Miranda."

"Miranda?" Mal sounded as confused as Wash felt. "Go back further."

"No." Instead Mr. Universe pulled another screen close and started working on that keyboard.

"Uh, please?" Mal asked, using his fakest sincere voice.

Wash, however, knew that Mr. Universe had found something, and he wouldn't go back further because there was no need.

The new screen showed a Fruity Oaty Bar commercial. Wash had been seeing that commercial for months, and its primary accomplishment had been to convince Wash to sample the products of Fruity Oaty Bar's biggest competitor. Based on the text on the bottom of the screen, this was what River was looking at right before she whispered "Miranda."

Then the commercial got all pixelated, breaking down into some kind of computer code that Wash couldn't begin to understand—that was why he stayed in touch with Mr. Universe, after all . . .

"Friends and potential lovers," Mr. Universe said, and Wash assumed the second part referred to Zoë, "I have good news and I have the other kind. Good is you're very smart. Someone *is* talking to her."

"The oaty bar?" Wash asked.

Mal got that determined look he got whenever he figured out that something was going to suck really badly for him. "Subliminal. It's a subliminal message broadwaved to trigger her."

Mr. Universe nodded. "I been seeing this code pop up all over, last few weeks. And I cannot crack it."

That got Wash's attention. He wasn't aware that there *was* a code that Mr. Universe couldn't crack.

"It's Alliance," Mr. Universe continued, "and it's high military, so here then is the bad. Someone has gone to enormous trouble to find your little friend. And found her they have." He looked at each of them in turn. "Do you all know what it is you're carrying?"

Wash let out a breath. They knew that River was at some kind of experimental facility disguised as an academy where they poked and prodded her brain repeatedly, that Simon had taken her from there and smuggled her to Persephone, and that the feds had been after both of them ever since. But sending guys like Dobson and attracting bounty hunters like Early was one thing. Sending subliminal messages into commercials?

That was a whole 'nother thing, and Wash wasn't sure he liked it.

"I believe," Mal said, "that we'd best get back on course."

"Haven?" Wash asked.

Mal nodded.

Simon went to check on River. They were leaving the moon belonging to someone who apparently really did call himself Mr. Universe. Kaylee told him that Wash knew him from a ways back and that was the only name he went by. *Every time I think the 'verse is as crazy as it can be, something comes along to prove me wrong.*

But then, Simon Tam was getting a little too used to being wrong. It had been stupid, he now realized, to ever ask off *Serenity*. Yes, River had been in mortal danger being on that job, but given the presence of Reavers, that danger would not have been alleviated had she remained on the ship. And Zoë had been right—River was the one who kept the situation from being far worse than it actually was.

Naturally, Captain Reynolds seized on Simon's rash decision and made it clear that he and River were no longer welcome.

However, for the moment, they were back on board, and headed for Haven. Perhaps seeing the miners and Shepherd Book would have a good effect on Mal. Simon had noticed that the shepherd had helped the captain keep a more even keel, and that not having the preacher around had a deleterious effect.

Simon entered the storage locker where River remained chained up, intending to clean her up. His heart fluttered, as he found himself reminded of the first time he saw her in Dr. Mathias's presence, in that awful chair with needles in her brain. This was more primitive than that chair, of course, but just as much a prison for her.

He wished he could unchain her. He wished that was an option.

She still had blood on her face from the fight in the bar, so he began by wiping her face. Staring at him, she said, "They're afraid of me."

"I'm sorry." The words sounded horribly inadequate to Simon's ears, but he could think of nothing else to say.

"They should be." Simon assumed she meant that they should be afraid, not that they should be sorry. She started to breathe faster. "What I will show them—oh God . . ."

Tears welled in her eyes, and her breathing got even faster, to the point where Simon feared she'd hyperventilate. Simon starting running his hand through her hair, trying desperately to comfort her. "It's okay, it's okay."

She started muttering. "Show me off like a dog, old men covered in blood—it never touched them, but they're drowning in it. So much loss . . ." Then she looked right at Simon instead of off into space. "I don't know what I'm saying. I never know what I'm saying."

Simon decided to venture a question. "In the Maidenhead, you said something. When you were triggered, do you remember? The captain saw you say something on the feed."

River nodded. "Miranda."

"Miranda." Simon had no more idea than the captain or any of the others had as to the significance of the name. Jayne had met a prostitute named Miranda once, but they all agreed that particular connection seemed remote.

Laughing bitterly, River said, "Ask her, she'll show you all."

"Show us what? Who is Miranda?" An awful possibility suddenly occurred to Simon. "Am I—talking to Miranda now?"

River gave him a classic little-sister look. "I'm not a multiple, dumbo."

"No, right." Simon was more relieved by her bratty choice of words than the meaning behind them, truth be told. "But I think somehow when they triggered you, it brought this up, this memory."

"It isn't mine. The memory. I didn't bring it, and I shouldn't have to carry it; it isn't mine." She looked at him urgently. "Don't make me sleep again."

"I won't." It was an easy promise for Simon to make. Had she not been in danger of shooting the captain, he wouldn't have done it the first time.

"Put a bullet in me. Bullet in the brainpan, squish."

Horrified at the thought—not in the least because there was more than one person on board who would do it without hesitation—Simon said, "Don't say that, not ever. We'll get through this."

She reached out and touched his face. It sent a shiver through Simon, as he realized it was the most directly affectionate she'd been to him since she left for the academy. "Things are going to get much much worse."

On the one hand, Simon didn't see how that was possible. On the other hand, Simon had felt that way in the past, and been proven very spectacularly wrong. In the face of that, he decided to go for blind optimism. "Well, the captain hasn't tossed us in the airlock, so I'd say we're—"

"He has to see," River said with sudden urgency. "More than anyone, he has to see what he doesn't want to."

It had been Simon's experience that Mal Reynolds didn't see *anything* he didn't want to. "River, what will Miranda show us?" he asked nervously.

River considered this. "Death."

"Whose death?"

Then River started laughing. It started as a quiet chuckle, then built into a louder guffaw, and then into flat-out crazy giggling. Between giggles, she screamed in his face: *"Everybody's!"*

Mal first came across Haven shortly after he acquired *Serenity*. He'd heard tell that a couple of his and Zoë's fellow Browncoats who'd disappeared wound up on that rock, and Mal had followed them to find out what happened. Turned out that the mining community thereabouts were willing to harbor the occasional fugitive for a small price. Since Mal had himself a boat, he offered to provide them with a ferry service on those occasions when it was required.

A few months back, they'd waved him, telling him that a thief was tired of running from the Alliance and wanted to settle down and do some honest work. Of course, thieving could be right honest work—it was all a question of who was being thieved—but Mal was willing to pick the young man up and bring him to Haven.

It was the first time they'd traveled yonder since Shepherd Book came on board. When they were fixing to depart, Book—who had announced his intention to depart *Serenity*—said that he'd be staying behind. Plenty of the miners were right spiritual folk, and welcomed the notion of a preacher in their midst.

Though Book had proven to be much more than the passenger he'd signed on as, Mal couldn't conjure a good reason to not let him stay, especially since the locals were so keen on him. And, truth be known, Mal wouldn't miss Book's praying overmuch. He'd has his fill of such foolishness, and left it behind on Hera.

Haven was pretty much a big mine and a small town. The mine looked like every other mine in the 'verse—big cave, lots of heavy equipment. Sadly, the town proved a powerful reminder to Mal of Lilac—several shacks, not as ramshackle as on the other moon, but indicative of the same hard living. They also had a church, which got more use nowadays, and a small vegetable patch, which was another of Book's contributions to the community.

One thing they had that Lilac didn't—and could rightly have used—was a large cannon, salvaged off a warship some years back. It was the main thing that kept Haven living up to its name.

Dozens of townsfolk came out to greet them, including Doane, who had cannon duty today. He jumped down from the chair that had been attached to the cannon and gave Mal a hearty handshake. Little Hiroko ran toward them at top speed, yelling "Aun' Kaylee! Aun' Kaylee!" at the top of his little lungs and crashing right into Kaylee's legs, giving them a fierce hug. Bernabe, one of the other Independents, gave Zoë a big hug that got Wash all fake-jealous.

And then there was Book.

Mal had little use for the preacher when he first

signed on. He paid his way with some cash, and also with some fruits and vegetables he'd taken with him when he departed Southdown Abbey and decided to, as he had put it, walk the world awhile. Seeing as *Serenity*'s crew lived most times on reconstituted protein, it endeared the shepherd to the crew something considerable.

Over time, Book had proven to be a lot more than just a shepherd. When Dobson revealed himself to be a fed, Book was the one who disarmed him, rendering him unconscious—and then, vexingly, refusing to let Jayne finish the job. There was Mal's rescue from Niska, during which Book showed a capacity for firearms that one didn't often find in the average man of God. And then there was the time Book got shot on Jiangyin; Simon had gone missing, and so they took the shepherd to a fed hospital, where one look at his ID got him VIP treatment, and *Serenity* on its way without a second glance after he got fixed up.

Now Book stood before Mal, a small smile under his silver goatee, his wild hair tied down in respectable cornrows. "Preacher," Mal said with a nod.

"Mal." Book returned the nod.

"Good to see you again. You look different."

The small smile widened. "Really? I'd say you look a mite worse. In fact, in my professional opinion, you all look like hell."

"That's what we all love about you, preacher, your ability to make us all feel good about ourselves." Everyone laughed at Mal's words, which defused any possible problems. The fact was, they *did* look like hell, which was hardly a surprise, but Mal wasn't ready to talk about it just yet.

Book looked to have got that, as the next thing he said was, "Well, as it happens, I think I have a salve for what ails you all." He grinned. "Dinner's in half an hour."

"Music to *my* ears," Wash said with a laugh of his own.

Soon they were all gathered in the communal kitchen, eating blessedly real food, and talking about everything and nothing. There was plenty of food, plenty of laughter, and plenty of joy, for all of which Mal was powerful grateful. Hiroko spent the entire time on Kaylee's lap, getting salad dressing all over his face and Kaylee's pants; the mechanic didn't seem to mind.

At one point, Jayne handed Book a box of cigars. "These're them Koobanes you said you like s'much. Fella I got 'em from on Boros says they're the best, and he ain't never steered me wrong in the past— mostly on account'a he'd know I'd cut him if he did."

Book gratefully took the box, and didn't even correct Jayne's pronunciation of "Cuban," which Mal found to be right neighborly. He knew they were named after a place on Earth-That-Was that produced cigars, and he recollected that Jayne carried on a fair piece after he found them on Boros, saying that the preacher'd been looking for 'em since he left the abbey.

Of all the people on *Serenity,* Mal would've put Jayne last on the list of people he'd expect to befriend the preacher, excepting Mal his own self, who had long since told the Lord to take a running leap. Yet Jayne and the shepherd had become fairly close, and Jayne actually almost got choked up when Book left, in a manner usually reserved for letters from Jayne's mother.

After dinner, Mal volunteered to help the shepherd clean up while everyone else went outside to watch the sun set and have what Bernabe called "the three D's": drinks and dancing and dessert. Jayne was eager for the first, Zoë and Wash for the second, and Kaylee for the third, and soon they were all outside with the others, leaving Mal and the preacher alone to discuss why Simon and River hadn't joined them for dinner. Simon was, of course, welcome, but he wanted to stay with River, and they couldn't afford to unchain her. "So," Mal said when he was done, which was right about when the recycler was full of all the dirty dishes, "that's when we thought coming here might not be such a poor move."

Book said nothing for several seconds, which Mal found unnerving. Then he said, "Let's join the others."

Mal wasn't sure what he was expecting from the preacher, but changing the subject wasn't it. "Shepherd—"

"Is something wrong?"

"That wasn't a confession, preacher—you may have cottoned to the fact that I don't rightly care for such notions. I wanted—"

"To fill me in. I'm filled. Now let me digest it a spell. Besides, I think the others might notice if we're gone too long." He smiled. "That *is* how rumors get started."

Unable to help himself, Mal laughed. "Gotta say, preacher, comin' here—it was something we all surely needed. Laughter's been in short supply on *Serenity* these days."

"I can imagine. Come."

The pair of them went outside. A campfire had already been made, though it wasn't wholly dark yet, and Jayne was picking on some instrument that the tin-eared Mal didn't recognize. As with dinner, Mal allowed himself to get caught up in it. He was able, for a spell, to forget about River and the Alliance and safewords and Fanty and Mingo and Lilac and Reavers, and just think about not thinking about anything.

He did, however, avoid the alcohol that was being passed around. Last time he got drunk at a celebration such as this, he wound up married to a grifter who almost destroyed *Serenity,* and Mal didn't fancy repeating that particular slice of history.

Later that night, most everyone had fallen asleep. Kaylee had gone back to *Serenity,* with a care package for Simon and River, while the rest of them took bunks in the town. Jayne and a few holdouts were still sitting around the campfire, Jayne's picking decreasing in quality in direct proportion to the increase in his drinking. Mal had thought that Book had retired, but then, as he wolfed down some leftover rice, he saw the preacher standing on a rise that overlooked where they all sat. Hauling himself up, he walked up the dirt path that led to the rise, shoveling rice into his mouth as he went.

As he got near, he heard Book's voice. Since there wasn't anyone else noticeable, Mal assumed he was praying.

"Lord, I am walking your way. Let me in, for my feet are sore, my clothes are ragged. Look in my eyes, Lord, and my sins will play out on them as on a screen. Read them all. Forgive what you can, and send me on my path. I will walk on, until you bid me rest."

Grinning, Mal said, "Hope that ain't for me, Shepherd."

As he got closer, Mal saw that Book was holding one of the Cubans. His prayer done, the shepherd lit the cigar. "It's a prayer for the dead."

"Then I *really* hope it ain't for me."

"It's for the men River might have killed in that bar."

"Weren't River that did it, you know that. Somebody decided her brain was just another piece of property to take—fenced it right up."

"You got a plan?"

Mal snorted. "Hiding ain't a plan?"

Shrugging, Book said, "It'll do you for a spell, and the folks here'll be glad of the extra coin."

Nodding, Mal thought, *I'd rather have been able to keep the coin*. A chunk of their Lilac takings was going to Haven in exchange for letting them stay a night or three. "But the Alliance'll be coming. They're after this girl with a powerful will. I look to hear the tromp of their boots any moment."

"You won't." Book put out his cigar, saving the rest

for another time. "This isn't a palms-up military run, Mal. No reports broadwaved, no warrants—much as they want her, they want her hid. That means closed file. Means an operative, which is trouble you've not known."

Now Mal understood why Book didn't want to have this conversation in the kitchen. *This'll fair ruin any chance of sleepin' well tonight—leastaways he didn't spoil the rest of the night.* "I coulda left her there. I had an out—hell, I had every reason in the 'verse to leave her lay and haul anchor."

"Not your way, Mal."

That amused Mal, in a bitter sort of fashion. "I have a way? Is that better than a plan?"

"You can play the thug all you want, but there's more to you than you're ever like to 'fess."

Mal shook his head. *First Fanty and Mingo, now the preacher. Everyone wants to crawl in my cranium today.* "You just think that 'cause my eyes is all sorrowful and pretty."

Book was polite enough to smile at the joke, then he grew serious again. "Only one thing is gonna walk you through this, Mal: belief."

"Sermons make me sleepy, Shepherd." Mal had more than a little tightness in his voice. "I ain't looking for help from on high. That's a long wait for a train don't come."

Sighing, Book said, "When I talk about belief, why do you always assume I'm talking about God?"

Mal had no answer for that. He just assumed, him being a shepherd and all . . .

No, that ain't fair to him. He's never shoved his God down my throat like a lot of his kind might.

"They'll come at you sideways. It's how they think: sideways. It's how they move. Sidle up and smile, hit you where you're weak. Sorta man they're like to send believes *hard*. Kills and never asks why."

As useful as Mal found this intel, he found its source to be peculiar—and it wasn't for the first time. "It's of interest to me how much you seem to know about that world."

"I wasn't born a shepherd, Mal."

That much, Mal had worked out on his own. "Have to tell me about that sometime."

Book looked out over the rise and said in a quiet voice, "No. I don't." Then he turned and walked off. "Sideways."

He left Mal alone on the rise with a whole lot of weight cramming down his mind.

—

River didn't like this dream.

Normally her dreams were chaotic and unfocused and confusing. Other people's dreams were like that, and River took comfort in the fact that her dreams made as little sense as everyone else's. It gave her a feeling of normalcy in a 'verse that had precious little normal in it.

But this dream—this dream was specific.

A normal dream didn't have a tactile or olfactory component. That was the weird thing. Her dreams always had plenty of sights and sounds, but never any of the other senses.

This dream, though, had her back in her classroom—the same one she thought about back on Lilac. Professor Rao stood at the front of the class, in front of a desktop screen that showed a single, dark planet, and all the students were sitting around her. But she couldn't just see Professor Rao, she couldn't just hear her words—she could smell the wood of the chair, the grass outside the tent where the class was held; she could feel the weight, small as it was, of the stylus in her hand, of the chair against her rear end.

This was wrong.

More wrong was that everything proceeded in a natural sequence. Cause and effect never mattered much in River's dreams; nor did the laws of physics. But this was *just like being in the class*.

It scared River as much as anything ever scared her.

Rao looked at her. "River? River, you look tired. I think everybody's a little tired by now. Why don't we all lie down?"

All the other children got up from their seats and lay on the floor next to their chairs.

What confused and frightened River was that *they didn't say a single word*. A room full of twelve-year-old children were constitutionally incapable of being that quiet when they moved, even if it was to take a nap.

The professor lay down as well. "A little peace and quiet will make everything better."

"No . . ." River managed to say through her fear.

146

"River, do as you're told. It's going to be fine."

But all River could see was the planet on Rao's screen. She didn't recognize it. And that didn't make any sense because she'd memorized the orbital visual image of *every single known planet* when she was seven. She could tell Ariel from Persephone from Jiangyin from Bellerophon. Not only that, but she'd memorized the nine planets that orbited the star in the sky of Earth-That-Was.

The world on Rao's screen didn't look like any of the forty-plus planets she knew about.

"Lie down," Rao said.

"No!"

River started awake, the heavy chains around her wrist in the storage locker. She saw Simon and Kaylee asleep next to each other against the wall, a plate with the crumbs from the food that Kaylee had brought from Haven sitting between them.

She wondered what the dream meant. It *had* to mean something. Dreams didn't just happen, and certainly dreams that *vivid* didn't happen unless there was a *very good reason*. She had to figure out why that planet—

With a start, she realized that she knew where the planet was. . . .

Wash had been surprised when Mal informed them that they wouldn't be staying on Haven but a day. He'd been hoping for more downtime, more opportunities to be alone with Zoë in a romantic—okay, mine shaft, but any port in a storm. Wash truly had no objections to the life he'd chosen on *Serenity*. There was a beauty to this ship that only a pilot could truly understand—or maybe a horseback rider, on account of she had a particular personality, and you needed to ride her *just* right.

But there were times when Wash desperately wanted to just run away with Zoë, to find some farm somewhere and just grow plants and raise a lot of kids and have several cats and dogs and just be people. Wash occasionally brought this up with his wife, who rightly pointed out that what Wash didn't know about farming was considerable, and that he knew more than she did, but Wash would usually point out that that's why they would have all the kids—so *they* could do the farming.

Zoë generally didn't buy that, especially given how small they'd start out as. That was when Wash usually just changed the subject.

Still and all, Wash was appreciative of the value of being on the move. In a lot of ways, *Serenity* was like a shark: had to keep moving, or they'd die. Of course, they weren't like a shark much any other way—no teeth, no fins, and a lack of ability to function under the water, but Wash never liked details to get in the way of a bad metaphor.

He was reenacting Mal's pathetic-yet-somehow-victorious swordfight against Atherton Wing on Persephone a ways back with his toy dinosaurs when the Cortex lit up with a wave from Inara.

That right there brightened Wash's day something fierce. It had been truly fine to see the good folks of Haven in general and Shepherd Book in particular again, and Wash had been sad to leave them—not just because they were good folks, but because their simple happiness and hospitality kept Wash's mind off the two fugitives they had on board. Not that Wash didn't like Simon and River—quite the opposite, not least because they annoyed Jayne so much—but the feds' tiresome insistence on trying to capture them did make life a lot more interesting than Wash generally preferred.

Abandoning the dinosaur sword fight—which wasn't working too well, on account of he didn't have any toy-dinosaur–sized swords—he activated the wave to reveal Inara's lovely face.

Were it not for Zoë, Wash could have fallen very hard for Inara. Then again, he didn't know many folk of either gender who wouldn't admit that she was the most beautiful woman in the 'verse. Luckily, Zoë was around to remind him of what he had with her—which was, primarily, a wife who knew several hundred methods of killing him, and that was *before* you put the gun in her hand.

"Inara! How's it going?"

"I'm fine, Wash." She was standing in an elegantly appointed space, looking like an old-fashioned tea house, with a gorgeous view of the mountains.

"Teaching the youth of the Alliance in the wild and wacky ways of copulation?"

Inara smiled, but it wasn't her usual indulgent smile whenever members of the crew got silly in her presence. It was the polite smile one gave to strangers one didn't wish to speak to, and Wash *knew* Inara wasn't like that with the *Serenity* crew—except Mal, of course.

"Everything okay, 'Nara?"

"Perfect, Wash. Couldn't be better. May I speak to Mal, please?"

Wash grinned. *No wonder she's rushing me off, she wants to talk to the good Captain Reynolds. This oughtta be fun.* "Surely and truly, 'Nara. Let me just get him up." Putting Inara on standby, Wash opened up an intercom line to Mal's quarters. "Mal? Mal, you there?" A pause. "Mal, you up?" Another pause. "Mal!"

"Whuh huh nuhwat?"

Chuckling, Wash asked, "You up? Got a wave. I'm'a bounce it down to you." Then he connected Inara's wave to Mal's quarters.

Normally, of course, decorum demanded that, once

the transfer was complete, Wash shut the wave down at the flight control.

But where would the fun in that be?

He kept Inara's image on the screen, and called up the feed from Mal's cabin on another. As usual when he was sleeping, Mal was shirtless, but still in his pants, a habit Zoë said was from the war, when you never knew when you'd need to be up and ready to fight at a moment's notice, a state of affairs that required one not to be struggling to hop into one's pants. However, the view only provided Mal from the bare chest up.

"Inara," Mal said, all nice and polite-like.

"Mal. I, uh—is this a bad time?"

Shrugging, Mal said, *"Good as any."*

"Please tell me you're wearing pants." Inara, of course, had the same view Wash did.

Mal grinned. *"Naked as the day I come cryin'. How's your world?"*

"Cold. It's autumn here."

Zoë came in, then. Wash waved her over. "C'mere, quick, darlin', we got us some theatre."

That prompted a raised eyebrow from Zoë, followed by her beautiful, wide smile when she saw what Wash was listening in on.

"Still at the training house?" Mal asked.

Inara nodded. *"Right where you left me."*

"I remember it as nice enough. Picturesque."

"It is that. What about you?"

Rolling his eyes at the incredibly lame small talk, Wash said defensively, "Hey, never said it was *good* theatre."

"Still flying," Mal said. *"So what occasions the wave? Not that to see you ain't—well, you look very fine."*

Jayne wandered onto the bridge. "What's all the gigglin' abou—"

Wash pointed at the screen, and Jayne just grinned.

Seemingly taken aback by Mal's compliment—not surprising, as such was a rare thing from the mouth of Mal Reynolds—Inara said, *"Oh—thank you. I—I guess we have something of a problem here. With the locals. I thought maybe—"*

"You could use a gun hand?"

Wash winced. The last time Inara had asked for that kind of help was on behalf of her friend Nandi. It was right after that that Inara announced her intention to depart.

"I'm hoping not. But if you were close at all, you—the crew—could take your ease here awhile. And there'd be payment."

"Payment is never not a factor," Mal said without any hesitation.

"Like hell," Jayne muttered.

"What's goin' on?" That was Kaylee, who then saw the screens before anyone could say anything. " 'Nara! She waved?"

"For the captain," Wash said. "We're eavesdropping."

"That ain't at all nice." Kaylee then grinned. "Move over, I wanna see."

"I could sound out the crew," Mal was saying. *"This pot like to boil over soon?"*

152

Inara considered. *"Soon. Not right away."*

Mal nodded. *"Well, it would be— I mean, I would like to— Kaylee's been missing you something fierce."*

They all groaned at that. Kaylee herself said, "Oh, they're so *pathetic!"*

"I miss her, too," Inara said with the first real smile she'd provided this whole wave. *"I even miss my shuttle, occasionally."*

"Yeah, you left a—got some of your stuff in a trunk. Never did get a chance to drop it off."

"I didn't mean to leave stuff."

"I didn't look through the—stuff." Mal sounded a bit defensive. *"Just sundries, I expect."*

Wash didn't believe either of them for a second, and based on the looks on his crewmates' faces, they didn't, either. In fact, a big smell was coming off this whole conversation.

"Well," Mal said after a moment, *"it's kind of late where I'm at. I'll send a wave as soon as I can."*

"Thank you."

And that ended that.

Wasn't but a few moments later that Mal sauntered onto the bridge, buttoning his shirt.

"Inara," Wash said, trying to keep a straight face. "Nice to see her again."

Zoë, typically, didn't beat around the bush. "So—trap?"

Mal nodded. "Trap."

"We goin' in?"

"It ain't but a few hours out."

153

Wash didn't like the sound of this. "Yeah, but remember the part where it's a trap?"

"If that's the case, then Inara's already caught in it. She wouldn't set us up willing. Might be we got a shot at seeing who's turning these wheels. We go in."

Much as Wash hated to admit it, Mal was right. They couldn't just leave her there with whoever was springing this particular trap.

Even though Wash knew in his gizzard that the trappers had some to do with them that was after River.

Kaylee asked, "How can you be sure Inara don't just wanna see you? Sometimes people have feelings." She smirked. "I'm referring here to *people*."

Mal looked at the four of them. "Y'all were watching, I take it?"

Wash considered hemming and hawing, but Kaylee just said, "Yes."

"You see us fight?"

"No."

"Trap."

Unable to argue with that logic, Wash then turned to the console and set a new course. He and Kaylee talked about going full burn for at least part of the trip, but several considerations wiped that from their screens. For one, they couldn't really spare the fuel, excepting an emergency, and this wasn't that—yet. For two, Kaylee had a few gadgets to put together as backup, and she needed time for that.

Four hours later, Wash had *Serenity* in atmo. Their approach vector had taken them in on the other side of the world from the training house, and Mal thought it best to fly in over ground rather than in orbit. Not that it mattered—Wash couldn't find anything in orbit aside from the same satellites that were there when they dropped Inara off.

Mal and Zoë joined Wash on the bridge as they got close. "We're about seventy miles from the training house," Wash said before Mal could even ask. "And nobody on radar. If the Alliance is about, they're laying low."

"They're about. Find us a home." Mal spoke with a confidence that Wash didn't share. The Alliance didn't usually do subtle. Fed ships were roughly the size of the average skyscraper on Ariel. They tended to announce their presence in the biggest possible way. If Wash didn't see a sign, he saw it as a sign that there was no sign for a reason.

Still and all, Mal was the boss, and Wash couldn't say for sure that the Alliance *wasn't* about, just that they didn't seem to be, so he looked for a proper landing site other than the training house's official one.

Mal turned to Zoë. "Remember, if anything happens to me, or you don't hear from me within the hour, you take this ship and you come and rescue me."

Zoë grinned. "What? And risk my ship?"

Heading for the exit, Mal said, "I mean it! It's cold out there. I don't wanna get left."

Wash chuckled mirthlessly as he set *Serenity* down in a handy gorge about twenty miles outside the training house. "So," he said to Zoë, "Mal's got a plan,

155

right? A brilliant strategy guaranteed to get Inara safely off with a minimum of fuss and a maximum of efficiency?"

" 'Fraid it's one of the captain's *usual* plans," Zoë said.

Sighing, Wash said, "That's what I was afraid of."

COMPANION TRAINING HOUSE

The operative watched.

Inara Serra was a truly beautiful woman, and not just in the sense that she was good looking—though she was that. She had grace and poise and brilliance and everything a sexual partner could possibly want. Probably more, truth be known, but he was sure she was able to adjust to the needs of her prey like the chameleons of Earth-That-Was. She knelt in front of a large Buddha statue that was the room's centerpiece, lighting incense sticks that gave the room a sweet smell that the operative was not especially interested in appreciating. The room was spare yet tasteful, much like its occupant. Had he any interest in such things, he likely would have sought out her services, given the appropriate occasion.

He had not let Serra out of his sight since he arrived at this training house. He had left the other Companions-in-training alone, as well as the other teachers. The only one who concerned him was Serra, because she was the only one who was connected to his mission. The parameters of that mission were clear, and he would not stray from them. To do so would be to violate the oath that had been programmed into him during his training.

Looking out the window of the chambers, he saw a line of young trainees filing by in robes, with red shawls pulled over their heads. Most were small, though he noted that the one in the back was a bit larger. The operative had seen several such processions since his arrival here a day ago, and he paid them no mind. They were also irrelevant to his mission.

Then the large one in the back broke off and came into Serra's chambers, kneeling down beside her.

"Dear Buddha, please send me a pony, and a plastic rocket, and—"

"Mal!"

The operative had to admit to being both surprised and amused—two states of affairs he rarely encountered in himself. There was a word in a long-dead language that came to mind: *chutzpah*. To actually disguise himself so ludicrously, and to actually get this far . . .

"What are you doing here?" Serra asked.

"You invited me," Reynolds said in a petulant tone.

"I never thought for a second you'd be stupid enough to come!"

Smiling, the operative thought, *Neither did I.* He had come to understand Reynolds's true psychosis in studying the man's file, but this showed him previously unrealized depths.

Still petulant, Reynolds said, "Well, that makes you kind of a tease, doesn't it?"

"You *knew* my invitation wasn't on the level—"

"Which led me to the conclusion that you must be in some trouble."

The operative nodded, enjoying watching this little drama play out. Serra had sent Reynolds the wave only because the operative made it clear that her ability to remain as a Companion would be jeopardized by the permanent damage he would inflict on various body parts should she not comply.

"I'm fine," Serra said unconvincingly. "I'm—giddy."

"For a woman schooled in telling men what they wanna hear, you ain't much of a liar."

"Mal, you cannot handle this man."

Seeing that as a good cue, the operative entered from his vantage point in the next room. "I have to say, I'm impressed that you would come for her yourself. And that you would make it this far in that outfit."

Reynolds stood up. "I can be very graceful when I need to."

Smiling, the operative said, "I've no doubt."

Serra picked out another incense stick, though the operative would have thought that the ones she'd burned were more than sufficient. Reynolds shed his absurd disguise and then asked, "What are you doing?"

"I'm praying for you, Mal."

The operative chuckled. "That's very thoughtful. But I mean it when I say you're not in any danger."

"Speak your piece." Reynolds spoke as if he were in charge, which the operative supposed was natural for a man who was used to leading people.

"I think you're beginning to understand how dangerous River Tam is."

Reynolds shrugged. "She is a mite unpredictable. Mood swings, of a sort."

"It's worse than you know."

"It usually is."

"That girl will rain destruction down on you and your ship. She's an albatross, Captain."

"Way I remember it, albatross was a ship's good luck—till some idiot killed it." At Serra's shocked look, Reynolds said, "Yes, I've read a poem. Try not to faint."

The operative nodded, conceding the point to Reynolds. "I've seen your war record. I know how you must feel about the Alliance."

In a tone that the operative would have, had he been anyone else, construed as dangerous, Reynolds said, "You really don't."

"Fair to say." The operative conceded a second point. "But I have to hope you understand you can't beat us."

"I got no need to beat you. I just wanna go my way."

The rallying cry of the Independents. "And you can do that—once you let me take River Tam back home."

As the operative moved about the room, he noted that Reynolds moved with him, always making sure to keep himself between the operative and Serra. The operative found that touching.

"No, no," Reynolds said, "you're working this deal all crabbed. You got to open with payment. Make a flush offer and then we'll see where this conversation goes."

The operative shook his head. "That's a trap. I offer money, you'll play the man of honor and take umbrage. I ask you to do what's right, you'll play the brigand. I've no stomach for games; I already know you'll not see reason."

Back in the almost-dangerous voice, Reynolds said, "Alliance wanted to show me reason, they shouldn't have sent an assassin."

Sighing, the operative realized that there was only one way for this to go. He had known that from the beginning, but he had hopes, nonetheless. "I have a warship in deep orbit, Captain. We locked on to *Serenity*'s pulse beacon the moment you hit atmo." That seemed to surprise Reynolds. The operative's Alliance ship had much better scan capability than Reynolds's heap, even modified as it had been by the young Kaywinnit Lee Frye, and the Alliance vessel was parked on the opposite side of the planet from *Serenity*'s entry vector, hidden from the *Firefly*-class boat's view.

The operative continued. "I can speak a word and send a missile to that exact location inside of three minutes."

Reynolds pulled a small device out of his pocket. "You do that, best make peace with your dear and fluffy lord."

"Pulse beacon." The operative sighed again. Reynolds was determined to unnecessarily complicate this.

"Advice from an old tracker," Reynolds said with a snide smile. "You wanna find someone, use your eyes."

"How long do you think you can really run from us?"

"Oh, a jackrabbit, me. 'Sides, I never credited the Alliance with an overabundance of brains. And if you're the best they got—"

"Captain Reynolds, I should tell you so that you don't waste your time: You can't make me angry."

Serra rolled her eyes. "Oh, please. Spend an hour with him."

Reynolds smiled at that, then his brain caught up with what Serra actually said, and mouthed the word, "Hey!" at her.

Were he someone else, the operative would've found that amusing. But were he someone else, he wouldn't be here. "I need her, Captain. River is my purpose and I will gather her to me. The brother as well. Whatever else happens is incidental in the greater scheme."

"Why is it that the greater scheme always makes everything not that great?"

"I want to resolve this like civilized men. I'm not threatening you—I'm unarmed."

The operative was fully prepared for what happened next.

Reynolds unholstered his gun and shot the operative right in the chest.

The impact, of course, sent him flying backward and to the floor. *So predictable,* he thought as he clambered to his feet and jumped Reynolds—who was trying to usher Serra out of the chamber. Getting Reynolds in a chokehold, he said calmly, "I am of course wearing full body armor. I'm not a moron."

He then tossed Reynolds against a wall, and used the momentum of that toss to block a blow from Serra. The move was a variation on a *kenshikai* karate strike, and the operative was impressed that she got as much power behind it as she did.

Not that it mattered, as he gave her a *uraken shome-nuchi* punch from the same discipline that put her to the ground in seconds.

Reynolds went for his gun again. The operative did a spin kick that sent both the captain and his firearm flying, then waited for him to get back up.

He did so, looking horribly unsteady, blood gushing from his nose. Had the operative kicked only slightly harder, he would have shattered Reynolds's nose, sending shards from the break into his brain, killing him instantly.

"No backup?" Reynolds asked in a voice that was more breathless than bravado, though he was obviously going for the latter. "We're making an awful ruckus."

"They'll come when they're needed."

"I'd start whistling."

"Captain, what do you think is going to happen here?"

Reynolds responded with a sloppy attack that the operative saw coming three seconds before the captain even moved. He effortlessly parried every clumsy blow

Reynolds attempted, returning with efficient simple punches and kicks of his own. Eventually, Reynolds fell to the floor right next to where Serra was kneeling, having recovered from the operative's blow, but not being quite ready to stand as yet. He did try to get up, but Serra, showing far more sense than Reynolds—which didn't take much—put a hand on his arm.

Taking advantage of this lull, the operative went to his briefcase and removed the sword. He hadn't wanted to sully the blade with such meager blood—Reynolds, though passionate, was nowhere near worthy of the blade—but enough was enough. "Nothing here is what it seems," he said to Serra.

"I know."

"He's not the plucky hero. The Alliance isn't some evil empire. This isn't the grand arena."

"And that's not incense."

The operative looked over at the stick that Serra had pulled out. It was burning away with greater speed than incense generally did.

Rather like a fuse.

Before even he could react, the operative felt as if a giant fist had punched him in the stomach, sending him flying backward through the doorway.

By the time he regained his bearings, Reynolds and Serra had, of course, left. *I should have kicked him harder.*

Four of his soldiers had come at the sound of the explosion. "Sir, what happened?"

"Just a flash bomb." He pointed in the direction the pair had run. "Go! Go!"

The quartet of armed and armored men ran to the stairs that Serra and Reynolds had made their escape down. The operative shook his head. *That was foolish. I saw the Companion only as a tool by which to bring Serenity* here. *I didn't account for her as a warrior in her own right—even after she used* kenshikai *blows on me, even though I knew of their extensive training, not only in lovemaking, but in deception.*

It was not a mistake he would make again.

——

Inara led a rather shaky-looking Mal down the corridor toward the staircase. Though her ears still rang from the flash bomb, she could still hear the footfalls of the Alliance personnel behind them.

Although she had confessed surprise at Mal's arrival, she wasn't truly shocked. If an incredibly stupid plan that had no chance of success was required, then Mal Reynolds was the man to implement it, and going up against that particular agent of the Alliance was stupid on a scale even Mal had rarely attempted.

Luckily for them both, she had been prepared. Life on the outer planets had bred in Inara a certain deviousness that, along with her Companion training, made having a flash bomb that looked like an incense stick second nature to her.

They arrived at the shallow staircase, and started running down. Mal was muttering something.

Her ears still ringing from the bomb, she couldn't make out his words.

"What?"

Mal shouted, "I think that I was winning!"

Somehow, Inara resisted the urge to club him over the head.

When they reached the bottom of the stairs, she stopped Mal and pulled a hidden lever that looked like one of the pieces of stonework. The section of the floor in front of the bottom stair slid open to reveal a trapdoor that hid the rest of the staircase. They continued down; once their heads cleared the floor, the trapdoor shut automatically. Moments later, Inara heard the footfalls of the agents running past, oblivious to the secret door.

Mal had been right about one thing—the Alliance didn't always breed their thugs for brains. While their leader was a force to be reckoned with, his hired help weren't likely to engage in the extralinear thinking that would allow them to determine where Inara and Mal had gone. For the next few minutes, at least, they were safe.

Three corridors presented themselves a few feet down the way.

"Where's the shuttle?" She assumed Mal didn't walk from *Serenity,* that even he wasn't stupid enough to park the ship anywhere nearby.

"What?" Mal asked at too loud a volume.

Inara repeated the question, louder and slower.

"Next to the mountain, outside the south entrance."

Nodding, Inara led Mal down the south corridor. It brought them to an exit halfway up the mountain in fairly short order. As they ran down, Inara saw that there were three guards on the shuttle. This distressed her, but Mal didn't seem surprised. He grabbed Inara, and they ducked behind a rock. Reaching into his pocket, he pulled out a grenade and activated it. A series of lights all around the grenade's circumference lit up. A second later, one light went out, then another.

"Isn't that a little extre—" she started to say, but Mal ignored her and tossed it down into the canyon.

It landed and bounced a few times, right at the feet of one of the guards, who saw it, instantly recognized it, and yelled, "Grenade!" He and the other two guards scattered.

As soon as they did so, Mal broke cover and ran for the shuttle. Confused, and concerned for her own safety, Inara ran after him, wondering why Mal would think running toward an about-to-explode grenade was a good idea.

She got the same answer she always got whenever she tried to comprehend Mal's thought process.

Arriving at the bottom of the canyon, Mal scooped up the grenade just as the last light went out.

Nothing happened. It was a dud. *Of course.*

One of the guards realized he'd been had and also broke cover, aiming his rifle at Mal. For Mal's part, he whipped out his own pistol and shot the guard down. By the time the other two reacted, Mal and Inara were in the shuttle.

Mal shooting gave Inara the opportunity to board first and climb into the pilot's seat. This was the same shuttle she'd rented, and she knew it a good sight better than the back of her hand. She also knew that Mal handled the thing about as well as a monkey who hadn't taken to flight training.

As she quickly plowed through the startup sequence, she said to Mal, "Hang on to something."

Looking peevish at her taking the pilot's seat, Mal asked, "You sure you remember how it—"

Inara lifted off, sending Mal sprawling to the floor. She tried not to smile. She almost succeeded. "I told you to hang on."

Sounding quite pained, Mal murmured from the deck, "I'm fine. . . ."

The course from *Serenity* was still in the navcom, so she was able to simply backtrack to the gorge where Wash had parked her.

Even as she approached *Serenity,* the ship's cargo bay door opened to allow six pieces of equipment whose haphazard construction had all the hallmarks of a Kaylee original to fly into the sky in six different directions.

Wanting very much to be angry—she was running away from the place where she was living, was teaching, was *happy,* dammit—she found herself feeling a thrill of sheer delight as she docked the shuttle.

It's like I'm coming home.

——

For the first time, the operative interfered with the training house beyond the confines of his use of Serra, but only insofar as he required a cup of tea, which the superintendent, a frightened woman named Sheydra, provided. *This is ridiculous,* he thought. *This should have ended already.* He activated his com and contacted Carmelito, who was back on the warship.

"Forget the pulse beacon." That was on the floor of Serra's room, doing him no good whatsoever. "There has to be another way to track the ship. Get a read on the navsat. It's a registered transport, you must be able to locate—"

"Sir?" Carmelito's tinny voice sounded over the com's speaker.

"Have you found a navsat trajectory?"

Carmelito hesitated. *"Sir, we've found seven."*

The operative sighed. He'd been sighing a great deal on this mission. "Does he think this is a game?"

He finished his tea and handed the cup to Sheydra. "Thank you, ma'am. I apologize for the disruption to your house." Giving her a bow, he then proceeded to his own shuttle. This world was no longer of use to him.

Within minutes, he was back on board the warship. Carmelito reported as soon as he entered the bridge. "We've tracked two of the navsats—they're decoys. Tracking the third now."

The operative nodded. It was likely a futile exercise, but fortune might favor them and provide them with *Serenity's* actual navsat. "Keep me informed. I will be with our guests."

He departed the bridge and went to the small space he used for interrogation. The air circulation wasn't at its best in here—it pumped in either very hot air or very cool air, depending on what the operative ordered—the lights were too bright, and the walls were featureless black. Crude techniques for putting one's subject on edge, yet quite effective ones.

The two prisoners were right as he'd left them—battered, bruised, tied up, scared. More crude yet effective techniques.

"We ain't done nothin'!" one twin cried as soon as the operative came in. The words were slurred owing to his missing several of his teeth.

"Mr. Mingojerry Rample. Mr. Fantastic Rample. Twins, born to Alanna Rample and an unknown father. One boy derives his name from a misremembered T. S. Eliot poem, the other from Alanna Rample's expression upon realizing she had a second bun in the oven. A thoroughly unimaginative woman, who passed that trait onto her sons." He sat down in the chair that faced the twins. "As to Mingojerry's statement, that is, in fact, incorrect. You've done plenty. There are eight warrants with your names on them. If you wish to continue living to violate those warrants, gentlemen, you will be so kind as to answer every single question I have regarding Captain Malcolm Reynolds and the crew of *Serenity*."

The latest dream picked up where the last one left off.

River was still in the class, the students and Professor Rao were still asleep.

But River was bleeding. Her head was bleeding, in each of the spots where they put needles in her, in each of the spots where Simon removed the needles when he rescued her.

She looked down at her desk. Its screen showed a display of the entire system, with each planet and moon linked by a white line.

Except for one.

Then the image closed in on that one planet, separate from all the others.

Hearing a sound, she turned to see that the entryway to the class wasn't the entryway to the class; it was a lab. River had seen plenty of labs in her time, most at the academy, but none of them looked like this.

Five well-dressed men stood in the lab, staring right at River.

Suddenly, she wasn't in class anymore, she was on the streets of a world she didn't know, surrounded by corpses.

Then she was in a house she'd never been in, surrounded by corpses.

Then she was in an office building she'd never been in, surrounded by corpses.

An entire world, full of death.

A blink, and she was back in class, breathing heavy, her stomach rising and falling so hard it almost bent her backward, the five well-dressed men just *staring* at her.

She turned, and a Reaver was standing next to her—the same one who crashed onto *Serenity* at Lilac. The Reaver grabbed her by the throat, cutting off her scream, opened his mouth, bared his razor-sharp teeth and moved in for the kill—

—and then she woke up, back in *Serenity*'s storage locker.

The chains weighed down her arms.

Leaning back against the wall, she cast her mind farther, just as she had done at Lilac.

Inara!

The Companion had returned. For the first time in so very very long, River allowed herself to feel joy. Inara's departure from *Serenity* had left a hole in the ship. It wasn't like when Shepherd Book left. On Haven, he found his home. Inara found her home on *Serenity* and stupidly left it.

She was with everyone else in the area outside Simon's lair, right near the passenger dorms where River and Simon slept.

Where River usually slept.

"We have every reason to be afraid." Inara sounded afraid, and she was. River could feel that she'd seen a man who scared her more than anything had in years.

"Why," Jayne asked, " 'cause this guy beat up Mal? That ain't so hard."

The captain was defensive. "He didn't beat me up," he insisted, even though River could see in Mal's mind that the man from the Alliance who scared Inara beat him up something fierce.

Inara answered Jayne's question. "Because he's a believer. He's intelligent, methodical, and devout in his belief that killing River is the right thing to do. I honestly think the only reason we haven't been blown out of the sky is that he needs to see her."

That confused River. *Needs to see me why?*

Simon asked, "Needs to see her why?"

River could feel Inara's struggle to articulate why she felt that way even as she came out and said, "I'm uncertain. I would say to be sure of the kill, but—I just know he'll kill us all to get to her."

A pause. "So no hope of a reward, huh?" That, naturally, was Jayne.

As usual, everyone ignored Jayne. Zoë asked, "Did he mention a deal of any kind?"

"Give the two of them up," Mal said. "Go my way."

Jayne said, "Which you was all ready to do not a day ago. What went sour?"

"Cutting them loose ain't the same as handing them over." Mal's distinction, River knew, would be lost on Jayne.

Sure enough: "That so? 'Cause the corpse I'm about to become is having trouble telling the difference."

Simon asked Inara, "Did he say anything about a 'Miranda'?"

Miranda.

River's eyes widened.

Miranda.

"What is that?" Inara asked.

"Don't know who or what," Zoë said, "but it's on River's mind."

Mal added, "Conjure it might be the reason he's after her."

Inara's mind was now turning to this, which helped her not dwell on the man from the Alliance who scared her so much. "You think maybe it poses some kind of threat to the Alliance?"

"Do we care?" Wash asked. "Are we caring about that now?"

Jayne was starting to get fed up, which was something that River knew would be bad for her and Simon. "You dumb-ass hogs, the only people she's a threat to is us on this boat!"

But River wasn't thinking about Jayne.

She was thinking about Miranda.

That's what it is.

She knew.

She understood.

And she was scared.

She had to let them know. Let all of them know. If they didn't know, they wouldn't understand.

The light in the storage room had a wire mesh on it. She clambered up the wall and started working on her manacles.

She couldn't just tell them. That wouldn't do it.

The others were arguing. Jayne was saying, "We take a shuttle, we drop her off, and we get 'em off our backs."

Zoë didn't let him finish before she said, "You think it stops there? What if they keep coming?"

"And what if she pops up again?" Jayne wasn't interested in what Zoë was saying—his words were mainly for Mal.

Inara's words were also. "You can't keep her in the storage locker forever, Mal. What are you gonna do when—"

"I don't know." And Mal truly didn't. He was conflicted. River had never felt such confusion emanating from Malcolm Reynolds, and it scared her almost as much as it scared him.

But not as much as Miranda scared River.

She kept working on her bonds.

" 'I don't know' is not a good answer," Inara said.

Mal didn't acknowledge that. "Look, we get back to Haven in a few hours' time—"

"Hiding under the shepherd's skirts," Jayne said with disdain, "that's a manful scheme."

Reaching his breaking point with Jayne, Mal snapped. "You wanna run this ship?"

Never one to equivocate, Jayne replied, "Yes!"

"Well, you can't!" Mal didn't equivocate much, either.

Jayne, though, got his mind on a roll, and he wasn't going to get off it now. "Do a damn sight better job'n you! Getting us lashed over a couple of strays." To Simon, he said, "No offense, Doc, I think it's noble as a grape the way you look to River—" Surprisingly, River felt that Jayne's words were true, which was probably the nicest thing he'd ever said to Simon. "—but she ain't my sister, and she ain't your crew." With that last, he was back on Mal. "Oh, and neither is she exactly helpless!" Everybody's mind was then filled with what happened at the Maidenhead. "So where's it writ we gotta lay down our lives for her, which is what you've steered us toward?"

Mal's reply was weak. "I didn't start this."

"No, the Alliance starts the war, and then you volunteer."

Jayne's words made something snap in both Mal's and Zoë's heads. Jayne was going down a very dark and dangerous road.

Typically, Jayne didn't even slow down. "Battle of Serenity, Mal. Besides Zoë here, how many—" Mal turned his back on Jayne, but he was too stupid to take that hint. "I'm talkin' at you! How many men in your platoon came out of there alive?"

Radiating more anger than River had ever felt from her, Zoë said in a quiet voice: "You wanna leave this room."

It was as nothing compared to what Mal was radiating. Names crowded his mind: Bendis, McAvoy, Baker, Grin, Johannsen, Tedesco, and so many more dead in that valley.

"You're damn right I do."

Jayne left, stalking up the stairs to the bridge level.

With his departure, the levels of anger lowered. But they remained present, particularly from Zoë and Mal.

Jayne had just ripped open a wound in both of them that had never quite gotten around to healing over proper.

Inara went to Mal, both physically and mentally. "This isn't the war, Mal."

"Are you telling me that because you think I don't know?"

"You came to the training house looking for a fight."

"I came looking for you."

River almost laughed. They were, in fact, both right.

"I just want to know who I'm dealing with." Inara was frustrated, as she often was in Mal's presence. "I've seen too many versions of you to be sure."

Again, River almost laughed. Mal wasn't that complicated, truly, but it was something she knew only because she knew what others didn't. Others might not cotton to it right off.

"I start fighting a war, I guarantee you'll see something new."

Mal left after saying that, but Inara followed him, which River knew he didn't want her to do.

"We'll get off." Unlike Simon's sadness when they were going to leave at Beaumonde, his determinedness now was out of sympathy for the crew. He didn't want to put them in danger. "River and I'll get off at Haven and find some—"

Kaylee had been sitting quietly nervous throughout all this, but now at the prospect of Simon and River leaving again, she said, "Nobody's saying that!"

Wash felt the need to amend that. "Nobody besides Jayne is saying that."

River kept working on the shackles. Only a little bit more to go.

Inara caught up with Mal in the cargo bay. "Mal—"

"I got no answers for you, Inara. I got no rudder. Wind blows northerly, I go north. That's what I am. Maybe that ain't a man to lead, but they have to follow, so you wanna tear me down, do it inside your own mind."

This time Inara was defensive. "I'm not trying to tear you down." Those words were only half true.

"But you fog things up. You always have—you spin me about. I wish like hell you was elsewhere."

"I *was*."

Neither Mal nor River could deny the truth of that—but River was the only one not denying several other truths regarding this pair.

Then River got out of the second shackle. She was free.

I have to show them.

Jayne opened the door to the storage locker before she could, saying, "No trouble now, little crazy person—we're going for a nice shuttle ri—"

She jumped him, taking him down with several blows to the head and neck. He fired a few shots, but she was within arm's reach before he could squeeze the trigger, so the shots went harmlessly into the storage locker. Then she closed the door, propped Jayne's body up so that the door wouldn't open, and hid her own smaller body behind Jayne's large one.

She felt as much as heard the others coming to investigate the shots. Mal arrived first and tried and failed to open the door to get at Jayne. "The other way," he said. "Find her and do not engage!"

He ran off. So did the others.

Simon stayed behind.

No, Simon, why did it have to be you? He could put her to sleep again.

Jumping out from behind Jayne, she startled Simon—but at least he didn't call for the others. She opened the door.

"It's gonna be oka—" was all he got out before she gave him a *nikite* strike to the throat, which took him out and kept him from calling for help or saying the safeword.

Just to be sure, though, she spun-kicked him to the ground.

Then she grabbed Jayne's gun and ran to the bridge, bolting the door behind her. They wouldn't be able to get to her until she had already done what was necessary.

Zoë was the first to the door, first to discover what she'd done. As Mal and Wash approached, she said, "She's sealed off the bridge. I do not like her there."

"Cap'n!" That was Kaylee, who tossed a bolt remover to Mal. He took it and started pulling bolts out of one of the wall panels.

River saw what he was trying to do: crawl in between the bulkheads and get to the bridge. She moved to the copilot's seat, brushed aside Wash's dinosaurs, and starting punching up coordinates on the Cortex screen. She had to find it, and then they'd all understand.

Soon enough, Mal's plan came to fruition. She

knew this, because one of the wall panels went flying off, and Mal himself crawled out from between the wires. Even as he lifted his gun, River—without looking at him, as her eyes were needed for her Cortex search—pointed Jayne's gun at him.

Mal's mind was filled with Kaylee telling them all what happened at Niska's outpost when River saved Kaylee's life. River didn't need to be looking at the three men she killed, and River's actions now were to remind him of that, at which they had nicely succeeded.

Just a few more seconds, I can find *the gorram thing . . .*

"The government's man, he says you're a danger to us." Mal was speaking plain, which River appreciated. "Not worth helping. Is he right? Are you anything but a weapon? I've staked my crew's life on the theory that you're a person, actual and whole, and if I'm wrong, you'd best shoot me now."

She cocked the gun.

"Or we could talk more," Mal added quickly.

Then, at last, she found it, punched it up on the screen. The very planet she saw in her dreams. The planet she had never seen before. The planet she wasn't supposed to know about.

The planet *nobody* was supposed to know about.

She pointed at the screen where an image of the planet spun slowly.

"Miranda."

Bernabe had been eating dinner when the Alliance ship came. In the time it took to chew two leaves of his salad, he heard explosions and screams that sent him suddenly back to the worst days of the war.

He'd put that behind him, he had. Was why he settled here, doing simple man's work. Found a lady to jump the broom with, had a pair of young'uns that swelled his heart near to bursting every time he laid eyes on them. Every day he watched his son and his daughter was every day he put the war further in the recesses.

Now it all came rushing back.

He ran out of the kitchen area to see half the buildings in the settlement were on fire. People were screaming in the streets.

And the sun was gone.

Blocking it was an Alliance vessel that made the worst ships Bernabe faced during the war look like that crapheap Mal flew. It swept over the town like a vulture fixing to chow down on a corpse.

Another sound like thunder came from behind Bernabe. He turned to see Doane at the cannon, firing.

The Alliance vulture was too fast by half, though, and his shot missed.

The sun came back as the Alliance ship swooped up, soon to come around for another pass.

Then Bernabe heard a familiar scream. His heart fair to stopped when he recognized it.

Mildred.

Of the dozens of townsfolk who ran through the streets, wounded, injured, dying, the only one Bernabe actually saw was his wife. Half her face was burned, and she didn't run so much as stagger.

"Mildred, what—"

"Babies . . . My babies . . . God, no . . ."

Bernabe looked up to see their home. It was an adobe hut that he and Mildred built soon after they got wedded.

Now it wasn't much more than a pile of blasted clay. And a grave marker for two beautiful children.

The sun went away again. This time, it was bullets that rained down, cutting people right and left in the streets. People screamed and fell, ammunition tearing through flesh in a manner that Bernabe had hoped to be leaving behind when he came here.

Bernabe turned to Mildred. "Get *down!*"

But he didn't see his wife. *Where did she—?*

Not wanting to, Bernabe looked down. Mildred lay there, bullet holes riddling her already-marred face. Bastards didn't even leave her pretty no more.

There were no shots from the cannon. Snarling with an all-too-familiar anger, Bernabe ran toward the cannon. "Gorrammit, Doane, whyn't you—"

Doane, though, didn't answer on account of he couldn't. He was just as dead as Mildred.

Bernabe fought in a brutal war. Throughout, even though he knew plenty who got wounded, and plenty more who died, he never got hurt his own self. Mal once called him a good luck charm, but Bernabe just figured he was good at ducking, was all.

So until this moment, he'd never felt a bullet rip through his flesh.

As he fell to the ground, his bizarre thought was, *Lot hotter than I figured . . .*

The bullet had gone through his back and out through his belly, and was 'round about what having a hot metal pipe shoved through your stomach probably felt like, though that, too, had never happened to Bernabe. To make up for it, he supposed, he couldn't feel a damn thing in his legs.

He did manage to roll over onto his back, though, and so he saw the man who shot him. It was some Alliance man wearing some kind of armor and carrying a pistol. He was now aiming it at Bernabe's head.

Guess I'll be joinin' you and the kids soon, Mildred.

Then the Alliance man fell down. Only then did Bernabe see Shepherd Book standing behind him with a mining tool he'd hit the Alliance man on the back of the head with.

Book then knelt down beside Bernabe. "Lie still, son—it's pretty bad, but we'll get you to a doctor soon-like."

"Shepherds ain't—supposed to lie." Bernabe could taste the blood in his mouth as he spoke.

A shot buzzed by—Bernabe felt it more than heard it. Moving remarkable fast, Book rolled over to the Alliance man he'd thumped, grabbed the same gun Bernabe had been shot with, and shot another Alliance man.

"Shepherds ain't—supposed to be—shootin' people neither." Bernabe knew that folks what came to Haven had pasts they didn't talk about—he knew that mainly on account of he was one—but a preacher who was a crack shot went beyond what he was expecting.

Without another word, Book ran over to the cannon. Gently removing Doane's body and laying it on the ground all respectful-like, he then leapt into the firing chair and whirled it on the Alliance ship just as it finished raining down fire on the shepherd's own church and adjoining garden.

Though Bernabe didn't rightly recognize the specific class of ship, he was familiar with the design type behind it. Was fair similar to the *Striker*-class that the Alliance favored during the war. This was souped up beyond all good sense, but Bernabe figured the engine core was in the same place.

He knew this mainly because Book's first and only shot went right to the spot on the undercarriage where Bernabe reckoned the core was.

Ship blew up a second later, crashing to the ground not too far from the cannon.

Shepherds ain't supposed to shoot down no ships. Bernabe was unable to make his mouth work no more, though, so was he stuck with just thinking it.

Which also meant Bernabe couldn't warn Book

about the man who was coming up behind him. The man, who wore funny glasses, struck Book in the back. Book didn't move after that.

"Impressive. I must confess, while I expected some minor damage, I hadn't expected this." Then the man's eyes widened. "Ah, Derrial. Given what I've read about you, this was the last place I expected to see you. And the last mode of dress, for that matter. Oh, you don't know me, so you don't need to widen your eyes like that. But I know *all* about you, which I daresay is more than can be said for the good people who have just died all around you. Or, for that matter, your former mates on *Serenity*." The man with the glasses sighed. "Under other circumstances, I might consider using the blade on you, but that is a thing of honor—and a man of the cloth shooting down a fully staffed vessel hardly qualifies as honorable. It barely qualifies as human." The man shook his head. "If only Captain Reynolds could see you now."

Then the man turned and walked away, signaling to somebody. Bernabe couldn't see who did the shooting, but he heard the shots—round about a dozen, all plowing into Shepherd Book who, thanks to whatever the man had done to his back, had to just be standing there and taking it.

He thought he saw Book fall to the ground, but it was hard to tell, as his vision was getting a mite fuzzy.

What distressed Bernabe most was the not knowing. Alliance never bothered Haven none—that was why it was such a haven. And Bernabe'd never seen the man with the glasses before in his life. That man knew the shepherd, true, but that didn't go much toward explaining anything.

Bernabe died on the dirt of his adopted home, never knowing why.

——

By the time *Serenity* was on approach to Haven, River had reopened the bridge and let everyone back in. Then she went on to explain herself, though her explanation didn't do much by way of enlightenment, to Mal's way of thinking.

Kaylee voiced the thought that Mal was sure was in everyone's mind—exceptng maybe Jayne's. "How can it be there's a whole planet called Miranda and none of us knowed that?"

"Because there isn't one," Mal said. He'd heard tell of Miranda some years back, but it took River putting two and two together afore Mal could come up with five. "It's a blackrock. Uninhabitable. Terraforming didn't hold, or somesuch. Few settlers died."

River was sitting next to Simon, looking a lot smaller than she was before. "I had to show them. I didn't know if you were going to make me sleep."

In a hoarse voice, thanks to River's method of disposing of her brother, Simon said, "You could've asked."

Suddenly, Kaylee looked like a lamp went off over her head. "Wait a tick, yeah! Some years back, before the war, there was call for workers to settle on Miranda. My daddy talked about going. I should've recalled."

Wash, who was back at the helm, guiding them

toward Haven, said, "But there's nothing about it on the Cortex. History, astronomy, it's not there."

Bitterly, Mal said, "Half of writing history is hiding the truth. There's something on this rock the Alliance doesn't want known."

Inara was peering at the screen. "That's right at the edge of the Burnham Quadrant, right? Furthest planet out."

Mal nodded.

"It's not that far from here."

Before Mal could agree both with that and the implication one step past it, Wash said, "Whoa! No, no."

Zoë seemed to concur. "That's a bad notion." She moved toward the copilot's seat.

"Honey," Wash said.

"I got it, baby."

"Show them the bad."

Mal frowned as he watched his first mate punch up some commands that pulled River's display back some.

Once he realized what he was seeing, Mal's crest fell a bit. *There's always something.*

Zoë explained to the others, who looked a mite befuddled, what Mal saw right off. She pointed at a dot on the display that corresponded to Haven. "This is us." She pointed to another dot, farther out. "And this is Miranda." Then she pointed at the empty 'twixt them. "All along here, this dead space in between, that's Reaver territory."

"They just float out there, sending out raiding parties," Wash added.

"Maybe a hundred ships. And more every year. You

187

go through that, you're signing up to be a banquet."

Mal gritted his teeth.

"I'm on board with the run-and-hide scenario, and we are just about—" Wash cut himself off. "Wait."

Turning to the window, Mal saw that they had long since entered atmo and were coming up on the mountain that overlooked the mining camp.

Or what used to be the mining camp.

The last time he was here, Mal made an enforced recollection of the similarities between Haven and what Lilac was before the Reavers came for a visit. Now, he had himself a second enforced recollection, as Haven now looked exactly like how Lilac wound up.

The buildings that weren't on fire, were out-and-out destroyed. Bodies littered the ground in a manner that reminded Mal a little too much of Serenity Valley—not much aided by Jayne bringing it to the front of his brain instead of the back where Mal generally preferred it.

An Alliance cruiser was grounded, due mainly to the engine core that was a pile of slag next to it. Mal suspected the work of the cannon—which, he noted, was the only thing on Haven still in one piece.

Wash didn't bother with the usual landing spot, instead setting down in the closest open space that would fit *Serenity*. Before he'd even completed the landing sequence, everyone, even Inara and River, had moved down to the cargo bay, waiting for Wash to set her down so they could find out what the hell happened.

Mal headed straight for the cannon, as did Jayne. Zoë moved toward the mine. Simon, his doctor bag gripped tightly in his fist, headed for the center of town, as did Inara. River moved more slowly, her bare feet barely making impressions in the dirt as she took it all in.

Girl her age shouldn't oughtta have to see this, was Mal's instinctive thought. *Then again, given what she has seen in her short time . . .*

Kaylee, meanwhile, was moving toward the burning church. "Shepherd? Shepherd Book?"

Then she stopped. Mal saw her look down, and then watched her face fall. Mal didn't need to look to know that it was Hiroko.

Nobody of no *age shouldn't oughtta have to see this,* Mal thought angrily as he ran to the cannon.

The first and only thing he noticed was the bloodied form of Shepherd Derrial Book, lying in a pool of his own blood, his body riddled with bullet holes, yet somehow still breathing.

To Jayne, he cried, "Get the doc!" but Jayne was off a-running before Mal could even get the words out.

Book seemed to be reaching in the air. Mal knelt down beside him. "Shepherd, don't move."

The preacher almost smiled. "Won't—go far."

Dammit, dammit, dammit. First Inara, then Book. "Shouldn't've been you. I'm so sorry, it was—they should've hit us—they should've hit me."

"That crossed my mind," Book said weakly. "I shot him down."

"I seen." Mal had actually figured Bernabe or Doane

or one of the others who got cannon duty would be the one to do the deed, but after all he'd seen, he couldn't bring himself to muster shock at the notion that it was Book who done it.

"I killed the ship—that killed us. Not—very Christian of me."

"I seem to recollect the phrase 'an eye for an eye' comin' from the Bible." Mal held his hand tightly. "You did what's right."

"Coming from you, that means—almost nothing."

Almost unwillingly, Mal smiled at that. Then the shepherd made an agonized noise of pain, and Mal held his hand even tighter.

"I'm—long gone . . ."

"Doc'll bring you around." Mal said it with enough force that he himself even was starting to believe it so. "I look to be bored by many more sermons 'fore you slip. Don't move."

"Can't—order me around, boy. I'm not one of your crew."

"Yes," Mal said, "you are." Folks may've set foot off *Serenity,* but you didn't never leave it. Mal knew that better than most.

Book started coughing up blood. Then he grabbed Mal by the shoulder, and stared into Mal's face, his eyes blazing. The preacher always had a philosophical calm about him, whether he was preachifying or fighting off Niska's thugs or Ranse Burgess's goons. Now, though, he was full of the fire and brimstone that Mal had always feared would accompany a shepherd on his boat, but which never came from Book.

"You—" He was almost hissing. "It's on you now—all this death, this shit—you have to find a course. *This* can't mean nothing. River—you have to—" The preacher faltered.

Gripping Book's hand with both of his now, Mal said, "Come on, keep it up!"

Book grabbed Mal's face with a bloody hand. "I don't care what you believe! Just—believe it. Whatever you have to—"

Then the preacher breathed his last. His grip slackened in Mal's own. His hand fell away, leaving a bloody handprint on Mal's cheek.

Jayne and Simon ran up a moment later, but it was too late. Mal could see on Simon's face that the doctor knew it, but he whipped open that bag of tricks of his and started working on the shepherd.

Mal got up and walked away. He didn't need to see death anymore, though there was plenty to go around. He saw Doane and Bernabe lying dead on the ground near the cannon as well. Doane was a musician who got on the wrong side of the law on New Melbourne. Bernabe was the good-luck charm of the Browncoats, a man who never once got himself shot.

And Book . . .

"How come they ain't waiting?" Jayne asked.

Mal turned to look at him, not comprehending.

"They know'd we was coming, how come they only sent one?"

Still uncomprehending, Mal looked to Zoë, who was standing near with Wash. Then her eyes widened. "They didn't know we'd come *here*." She turned to

Wash. "Get on the Cortex, wave the Sanchez brothers, Li Shen—anyone who's ever sheltered us after a heist. Tell them to get out—get out *now*."

Then, finally, Mal put it together. That bastard with the glasses didn't attack Haven because they were coming here—he attacked because they *might*.

——

Half an hour later, Mal sat alone on the bridge of his boat. Every single place Wash called either didn't answer, or barely did. All of their safehouses were destroyed, just like Haven. Somehow that man—Book had referred to him as an "operative"—had learned about them, and took them down, all of a piece.

"I'm sorry."

Whirling toward the com screen in surprise, Mal saw the face of the man with the glasses. Of all the unmitigated gall, this, to Mal's mind, was the unmitigatedest. Not just to call, but to *apologize?* "You—what?"

"If your quarry goes to ground, leave no ground to go to."

Mal had carried hate for a lot of folks in his life, but it was as a weak candle compared to his hatred for this person whose name he did not even know. To sit there and philosophize after killing good men like Doane and Bernabe and Book, after murdering children . . .

"You should have taken my offer—or did you think none of this was your fault?"

"I don't murder children."

Calm as ever, the man said, *"And, as you can see, I do. If I have to."*

Mal sat up. "Why? Do you even know why they sent you?"

"It's not my place to ask. I believe in something that is greater than myself. A better world. A world without sin."

Unable to get his brain around the notion that killing children provided a world without sin, Mal instead asked, "So me and mine got to lie down and die so you can live in your better world?"

The man looked at Mal like he was tweaked. *"I'm not going to live there. How could you think—? There's no place for me there, any more than there is for you. Malcolm, I'm a monster."*

That was the first thing the man said in Mal's presence that he agreed with.

"What I do is evil, I've no illusions about that. But it must be done."

"Keep on talking. You're not getting a location trace off this wave." Mal suspected that the man knew that—that was the first trick you learned in this game.

"And every minute you keep River Tam from me, more people will die."

"You think I care?" The bravado sounded false even to Mal's own ears.

"Of course you do. You're not a Reaver, Mal, you're a human man and you will never—"

That was the second time this gentleman had called Mal by his first name without permission, which was

193

twice more than Mal was appreciative of. So he cut him off, as well as all the other screens.

He sat in the dark bridge for several moments.

Then he called River's image of Miranda back up.

"There's something on this rock the Alliance doesn't want known."

"You're not a Reaver, Mal."

"They'll come at you sideways."

Mal stared at Miranda for a spell. Then he got up.

Time to do a little sideways moving of my own.

Outside, the others were gathering the bodies near where Book died, by both the cannon and the broken hull of the Alliance ship, laying blankets over them. That wasn't to last much longer.

"Get these bodies together," Mal said.

"We got time for grave digging?" Zoë asked.

"Zoë, you and Simon are gonna rope 'em together. Five or six of 'em. I want them laid out on the nose of our ship."

Simon's mouth fell open. "Are you insane?"

"What do you mean, the bodies?" Kaylee asked in confusion.

"Kaylee, I need you to muck the reactor core, just enough to leave a trail and make it read like we're flying without containment, not enough to fry us."

However, Kaylee was still back on the bodies. "These people are our friends."

Mal wasn't in a mood for justifying right present. "Kaylee, you got a day's work to do and two hours to do it." He turned to Jayne. "Jayne, you and Wash hoist up that cannon mount. Goes right on top. Piece or two of the other ship, stick it on. Anyplace you can tear hull without inner breach, do that, too." He looked around. "And we're gonna need paint. We're gonna need red paint."

Inara started muttering a prayer in Chinese.

Zoë had her sir-you've-lost-your-rutting-mind look. "Sir, do you really mean to turn our home into an abomination so we can make a suicidal attempt at passing through Reaver space?"

That's our Zoë, never beatin' 'round no bushes. "I mean to *live*. I mean for *us* to live. The Alliance won't have that, so we go where they won't follow."

"God's balls," Jayne said, "there's no way we're going out there!"

Everyone started talking at once, some in English, some in Chinese, all of it of no interest to Mal. He saw movement in the Alliance hulk behind everyone who was facing him and jawing.

When he pulled his gun, everyone shut up.

"This is how it works. Anybody doesn't wanna fly with me anymore, this is your port of harbor. There's a lot of fine ways to die. I'm not waiting for the Alliance to choose mine." As he spoke, he walked past his crew toward the ship. The movement was an officer of some type, struggling to clamber out of the wreck. Upon seeing Mal, he raised his hands in surrender.

Mal shot him in the head.

He turned back to his crew. "I mean to confound those bungers, and take my shot at getting to Miranda, maybe finding out what-all I'm dying for. That's the only path I see left and I got to walk it. So I hear a word out of any of you that ain't helping me out or taking your leave, I will fucking shoot you." He picked up the body of the man he'd shot and then dropped it at Zoë's feet. "Get to work."

When Mal Reynolds first set eyes on *Serenity*, it was love at first sight. The dealer was trying to sell Mal on a clapped-out hauler that had been given a new paint job to disguise the fact that it was but a few light-years from falling into tiny pieces.

Off on the side was a *Firefly*-class ship. It wasn't even with the others for sale on account of it being no more spaceworthy than the mountains behind it. The dealer had gotten it cheap and was going to scrap it for parts, but Mal made him a good offer, and the dealer, being more greedy than foolish, took it.

Now, as Zoë had said, they were making it an abomination. She and Simon strapped the bodies of the good folk of Haven—who, Mal was the first to admit to, deserved finer—to the front, like figureheads on sailing ships of old. They'd made sure to take the bodies that were most defiled. At Mal's request, they put one in a spacesuit and lashed it to the cannon, which Jayne and Wash had mounted. No self-respecting Reaver ship would go into the black unarmed. The two of them had also torn the hull in several select bits and welded parts from the downed Alliance ship, as well as bits of mining equipment, to the outside.

Cursing and swearing and whimpering the entire time, Kaylee modified the engine. Mal knew it was like asking Kaylee to slice open her own wrist, but he also knew that none else but she could do it proper.

Mal himself took to painting it. He'd seen plenty of Reaver ships in his time, and knew the pattern: corruptions of Chinese characters and figures that Mal himself didn't know, but which River said was reminiscent of war paint of certain American tribes on Earth-That-Was.

When they were done, Wash took off, setting a course for Miranda.

No one spoke as they broke atmo. *Serenity* was as quiet as a tomb.

Wash sat at his post, making sure that the radiation readings stayed Reaver-like, and that the actual leakage wasn't fatal to all of them. Zoë and Jayne were in the dining room, silently checking their weapons. Kaylee was, like Wash, keeping a close eye on the engine. Simon was in the infirmary, mixing tubes or somesuch. Proving that one shouldn't underestimate the drawing power of being crazy, River was fast asleep in her bunk—there seemed little point in chaining her up. *Maybe it isn't that she's crazy—maybe it's just that, with everything in her head, turning* Serenity *into a Reaver ship ain't exactly top of the list of bad shit goin' down.*

The only person unaccounted for was Inara, who was in what used to be her shuttle. Mal found himself walking up to the hatch.

"Mal," Inara said from the corner, causing him to jump. She was going through the trunk she'd left behind.

"Didn't see you," he said.

"I figured that."

"Anything of use in there?"

"Maybe."

She got up and crossed over to the bed, which was no longer adorned by the silk and satin Inara favored, but instead the good old-fashioned battered flannel that came with the shuttle. They both sat on it.

Mal actually liked this. It was almost like it was a normal day. Add a few curtains and burn some incense, and it would be like the last six months never happened.

"You don't have to stay in the shuttle, you know," he said suddenly. "There's empty rooms, if you wanna sleep awhile." Of course, one of those was Shepherd Book's old room . . .

"You think anyone's set to sleep?"

Mal smiled, thinking of River.

"Simon's portioning out overdoses of morphine, just in case."

So that's what he's doing in there. "Cheerful fellow." He looked around. "Did you really miss this place?"

"Sometimes." She smiled ruefully. "Not so much right now."

Unable to look at her, he asked, "Why did you leave?"

She *did* look at him. "Why didn't you ask me not to?"

Mal couldn't answer that. Or, rather, he could, but not in any satisfactory manner. So, instead, he got up. "I, uh, I'd better go check on the crew. See how the inevitable mutiny is coming along."

He took his leave quickly.

SERENITY

Everybody was on the bridge of *Serenity*.

Nobody spoke a word.

Wash piloted the ship through the dead space that
Reavers tended to dwell in. He flew the ship hard and
fast. Any sign of caution would give away their disguise. Wash was never nervous when he flew, but he
was nervous now—not because he doubted his own
skills, but because he had some notion of what would
happen should they be discovered.

Zoë stood at her man's back, a comforting hand on
his shoulder, wishing him all the strength she had so
that they would get through this in one piece. Zoë
didn't much fancy feeling helpless, but right now all
she *could* do was stand and watch while her husband
did all the work. She had done what she could—swal-
lowing bile the whole while—to make up *Serenity* like
it belonged around these parts, and now it was up to
Wash.

Jayne was never much for praying, though he did
believe in God—and that he himself was going
straight to hell. That didn't matter none to him. Way he
figured, all the fun folk to be with was gonna be there

with him. What he did give some caring to was the manner in which he arrived, and he didn't want it to be 'cause of no Reavers. So he prayed.

Kaylee winced every time she heard *Serenity*'s engine whine or burn too loud or do whatever such thing as it might do when it was broke. It was bad enough when she sounded like that on her own because of, say, the captain not letting Kaylee replace the entry couplings, but to know that she did it purposeful was like tearing out her own heart. She just hoped this was worth it, was all.

Inara had thought she had put all this behind her when she left *Serenity*. She'd seen so much death since coming on board, and she had thought that that part of her life would be closed once she disembarked. Yet how could she deny the thrill she felt, the joy at being back with these people? *After all, if I wanted safe, I would've remained on Sihnon in the first place.*

Simon thought about all the bodies back on Haven, and the others the crew learned of soon thereafter. Some were places he knew, others ones that they hadn't visited in the eight months since Simon came on board. But they were still people who died because of him. True, it was that man who beat up the captain who did it, but it was Simon's own actions that started the chain of events that led to those people's deaths. A lifetime ago on Osiris, Mother had asked him if he was going to throw away everything he'd worked for his whole life. He'd been prepared for that, and had deemed rescuing River from those who would experiment on her, operate on her, torture her, to be worth it.

But was it worth all the *other* lives? Was River's life worth Shepherd Book's? He had no answer.

Mal stared straight ahead into the black. *Ain't nobody here but us Reavers,* he thought emphatically at the ninety-odd broken and violated ships that littered this little piece of the black. He needed to get to Miranda, find out what it was that led a man to kill preachers and children and crooks alike. The Alliance had always been about control, and Mal had always been against it—but this was extreme even for them. And now Mal's life literally depended on his finding out why.

River knew all these things. And she knew something else. Nobody wanted to give her up. Not even Jayne, anymore. He still didn't want her on the ship, but Jayne wouldn't give River up to someone who would do what the Alliance operative did. Even he had standards, such as they were.

And that made River happy. Despite what Captain Reynolds may have said, *Serenity* was home—even all gussied up like Reaver craft. And *Serenity* would keep her safe.

Minutes later, they were past the Reaver armada, having gone through the gauntlet unmolested. Minutes after that, they arrived at Miranda.

MIRANDA

Inara stood on the bridge, entranced by clouds.

They were in Miranda's atmosphere, but the cloud cover was intense in the area they were descending into, so they couldn't see anything. At one point, she looked at Wash and asked, "Why don't we just go down in a different part of the planet?"

Normally, this would've prompted a grin from Wash, but the last few days in general and the current physical state of *Serenity* in particular made it impossible for even the jovial Wash to express that much glee. He did, however, provide a half-smile. "I could go on for half an hour with some *really* boring flyboy jargon about approach vectors and descent trajectories and launch windows and the relative positions of Haven and Miranda, but the short answer is, it'd add about three hours to our arrival time and be more trouble than it was worth."

She smiled back. "Fair enough."

Zoë looked up from the copilot chair. "Every reading I'm getting says normal. Oceans, landmasses—no tectonic instability or radiation."

Inara frowned. That didn't make sense for a world that terraforming didn't take to.

"Yeah," Wash said, "but no power, either."

"Nothing at all?"

Before Wash could affirm that, something caught his eye on one of the screens. "Wait. Something." He looked briefly up at Mal. "Might be a beacon, but it's awful weak."

"Find it."

Wash nodded and homed in on the signal. "I got it. Changing course—we should be able to land about three klicks from it."

Mal looked at Zoë and Jayne. "Let's suit up."

Inara followed them down to the cargo bay. Silently, she and Kaylee and Simon helped Mal, Jayne, and Zoë, respectively, suit up. Even though Zoë didn't find anything to indicate that the terraforming hadn't taken, didn't mean it wasn't so. Best to assume nothing out there was breathable.

Kaylee opened the inner door after they landed. Mal, Zoë, and Jayne stepped through it. Inara heard Wash's work boots clang on the metal of the stairs as he came down from the bridge. Nobody was saying a word, but everyone wanted to know what was out there.

Once the inner door closed, Kaylee opened the ramp, and the three of them stepped out. Their radios were tied into the speakers in the cargo bay, and Inara could hear them speak.

"Gravity's Earthnorm." Mal probably gleaned that just from walking a step or two.

"O$_2$ levels check," Zoë said, *"pressure—if there's anything wrong, the scanner isn't reading it."*

Inara heard the click of a helmet seal breaking. Mal's voice sounded less tinny when he said, *"Well, something sure as hell ain't right. And those buildings're a mite taller'n advertised. Kaylee, let us back in."*

Kaylee opened the inner door, and the threesome reentered. Inara wondered how there could be tall buildings. *Probably the same way there's breathable air.*

Once Mal, Zoë, and Jayne were out of their cumbersome suits, all nine of them exited the ship. Inara did everything she could to avoid looking at the violated ship as she stepped down the ramp—which turned out to be easier than expected, as Mal had undersold Miranda in his report.

There weren't just a few tall buildings. They were in a massive city, as big, as sprawling, as *modern* as anything on a central planet.

But it was something else that made it very much unlike the worlds on which Inara had grown up:

Quiet.

Some of the buildings were obviously decimated by now-long-gone-cold fires. Much of the city had been overgrown by weeds and other plant life.

But there was no sign of any kind of animal life. Not even insects or birds.

"This ain't no little settlement," Jayne said.

"We flew over at least a dozen cities just as big," Zoë said. "Why didn't we hear about this?"

Mal pointed. "Beacon's up ahead."

They started walking through the town. Inara had never seen anything like this. She'd been in retreats and to gardens and estates that were this quiet, but even there, it was the silence of nature, the silence of solitude. This was wholly unnatural.

When they entered a dark tunnel, lights came on automatically, triggered by their movement. *Whatever happened here doesn't seem to have affected all the machinery.*

"Ho," Zoë said, kneeling down. Inara followed her movement to see a skeleton, facedown on the ground, clothes tattered. Zoë started examining the body. "No entry wound, no fractures . . ."

Mal hazarded a guess. "Poison?"

Zoë shrugged.

They moved on, up a flight of stairs to a walkway that looked out over the dead city.

Inara shivered. That was something else this quiet was: cold.

As Mal passed under an unlit banner, it suddenly did light up—for a moment, with an ad Inara hadn't seen in at least a decade. Then it sputtered and died. *Didn't affect the machinery, but it hasn't been maintained, either.*

Jayne approached a downed hovercraft. "Got another one!"

They all followed. The last thing Inara wanted to see was more evidence of death in this place that seemed to personify death, but she found she couldn't turn away, either.

She saw two skeletons, one an adult, one a small child. Like the person Zoë found, there was no sign of violence, no damage to the craft. They were strapped into their chairs as if nothing was wrong.

"They's just sittin' here. Didn't crash." Then he got up. "Couple more here."

Inara couldn't look anymore. She turned to River, to see if this was, as hoped, providing some answers for her own problems.

If they were, it wasn't obvious. River looked as agitated as Inara had ever seen her, and she'd seen her in some pretty crazed rages.

"Kaylee, come this way. Come here. Don't—" That was Simon. He was trying to lead Kaylee away from an office building window.

With a start, Inara saw why.

So did Kaylee, who screamed, "*Gaaaa*—oh, God!" at the sight of a blue-faced corpse pressed up against the glass.

At Kaylee's scream, everyone—except River— came to get a closer look. Simon peered in closest, probably to try to determine how they died.

What startled Inara was that all the bodies they saw in the window were comfortable. Sitting, leaning, lying down on their backs. If not for the mild decomposition, they'd have looked like they were sleeping.

"How come they're preserved?" Jayne asked.

Mal looked up. "Place must've gone hermetic when the power blew. Sealed 'em."

"What're they doing?" Kaylee sounded as upset as River looked. "What's everybody doing?"

"There's no discoloration," Simon said. "Nobody's doubled over or showing signs of pain."

"There's gases that kill painless, right?" Mal asked. Simon nodded.

Inara said, "But they didn't fall down. None of them. They just *lay* down."

"More than anything," Simon said, "it looks like starvation."

Mal snorted. "Anybody want to bet there's plenty of food around?"

"They just lay down . . ." Inara couldn't wrap her mind around it. She could see people dying in their sleep, but not like *this*. This was—

She didn't know what it was, but it sickened her.

Suddenly, River dropped to her knees and started screaming. *"Renzi de Shang Di, qing dai wa zhou,* make them stop, they're everywhere, every city, every house, every room, they're all inside me, I can hear them all, and they're saying *nothing!* Get up! Please, get them up! *Wo shang mei er, mei xin, bian shi tou,* please God make me a stone . . ."

"She's starting to damage my calm," Jayne said. Inara wondered how any of them could possibly have any calm left to damage.

"Jayne—" Zoë started, but he wasn't done.

"She's right! Everybody's dead! This whole world is dead for no reason!"

His calm refreshingly undamaged, Wash said, "Let's get to the beacon."

They kept walking in silence, save for River muttering to herself in both English and Chinese as she walked alongside a protective Simon, until they reached a landing strip. At the end of it was an Alliance research vessel, of a type still in use, but which Inara realized was about ten years old, based on the design. They didn't have those fins anymore, for one thing.

Unlike the other downed craft they'd seen, this one was damaged, badly.

Cautiously, Mal, Jayne, and Zoë going in first, the others following when they said it was clear, they all stepped inside.

The ship was a mess. Doors were pried open, clothes and possessions strewn about the floor, damage to the bulkheads—but no bodies here.

River had stopped muttering when they came inside. Breaking away from Simon, she approached one particular console and turned one control on it.

A hologram sprung to life in the middle of the room. It was a woman in an Alliance uniform. She looked frightened.

"—just a few of the images we've recorded, and you can see it isn't—it isn't what we thought. There's been no war here, and no terraforming event. The environment is stable."

She spoke as if that would be a revelation. Given their reactions upon landing, she had reason to think so.

"It's the Pax—the G-32 paxilon hydrochlorate that we added to the air processors. It's—" The woman started to cry. "—well, it works. It was supposed to calm the population, weed out aggression.

Make a peaceful— It worked. The people have stopped fighting."

Inara's stomach lurched as she realized what happened.

The woman's next words confirmed it: *"And then they stopped everything else. They stopped going to work, stopped breeding . . . talking . . . eating . . ."* She took a deep breath, obviously trying to keep her emotions in check. She was succeeding about as well as Inara, who could feel the tear run down her own cheek. *"There's thirty million people here, and they all just let themselves die. They didn't even kill themselves. They just—most starved. When they stopped working the power grids, there were overloads, fires— people burned to death just sitting in their chairs. Just sitting."*

Inara jumped at a loud banging sound, then calmed when she saw the woman react to the same thing—it was from the recording.

"I have to be quick. There was no one working the receptors when we landed, so we hit pretty hard. We can't leave. We can't take any of the local transports, because—" The bang came again. *"There are people—they're not people. About a tenth of a percent of the population had the opposite reaction to the Pax. Their aggressor response increased beyond madness. They've become— They've killed most of us—not just killed, they've done—things."*

Another tear rolled down Inara's face, as she realized that her naive belief of only moments ago that things couldn't be any worse was so much idiocy.

209

Wash spoke the words they were all thinking. "Reavers—they *made* them."

"I won't live to report this, and we haven't got power to—people have to know." The woman broke down again. *"We meant it for the best—to make people safer—to— God!"*

As she spoke, the door behind her broke down. The woman whipped out a gun and fired at the direction of the noise. Then she put the gun to her own head.

Before she could pull the trigger, a creature instantly recognizable as a Reaver jumped her, biting at her and tearing at her clothes and flesh.

"Turn it off," said a disgusted, tiny voice. To Inara's surprise, it was Jayne, who looked as pale as Inara had ever seen.

They all did.

Wash shut the playback off.

Mal turned and exited the craft. Inara followed him without hesitation. Before he said he had no rudder, but right now he was hers. She was born and raised in the Alliance, believed in it. She had supported unification during the war, felt that the 'verse was better off with one unifying authority instead of several small, fractious ones. More than anything else, Inara believed in peace, and she had thought that was only to be achieved through centralized authority.

Until now.

Now she saw what that authority was capable of. Worse, she saw peace taken to its extreme. And it was the most awful thing she'd ever seen.

Mal was standing, looking down the airstrip at the

dead city in the middle of a dead planet. Wrapping his arm around her at her approach, he held her close for support. She put her hand over his. Right now, she desperately needed his presence, his strength, or she would go as mad as a Reaver.

In a quiet voice, sadness etched in every syllable, Mal spoke. "I seen so much death. I been on fields carpeted with bodies, friends *and* enemies. I seen men and women blown to messes no further from me than you."

Inara started, "Mal—" but he needed to say this, and went on.

"But every single one of those people died on their feet. Fighting. Or hell, running away—doing summat to get through. This is—"

Tears now streaming down her cheeks, Inara said, "Mal, I need your help with this. I need you to help me, because I can't—"

Mal pulled her into his arms, brought her face to his. They didn't kiss, but they *touched,* needing to feel each other's living, breathing selves.

They needed to know that they were each alive.

— —

Simon was no stranger to death—or so he had thought. He had seen plenty of death in his time as a surgeon, done plenty of autopsies, but death in a hospital, even the chaotic environment of an emergency room, had an antiseptic quality.

The first dead body he ever encountered outside a hospital or funeral service was on *Serenity.*

All the bodies he'd seen—from the guard on Ariel that Jayne killed when they escaped Alliance custody, to Mal and Zoë's war buddy Tracey, who in essence Simon saw dead twice, to the bodies River left behind in the Maidenhead—had been ugly and messy and unpleasant and scary, but Simon was starting to at least grow accustomed to it, if not inured to it.

What he saw on Miranda, though . . .

He broke out of his shocked reverie when River fell to her knees and started vomiting on the floor.

Jayne muttered, "Smartest thing I ever seen that girl do."

Simon put his hand on her back, let her ride it out. After the last heave, he prompted, "River?"

"I'm all right."

She looked at him, and Simon saw something he hadn't seen since River first departed the Tam estate on Osiris for the academy.

He saw his little sister.

Among the many sins visited on River's brain by Dr. Mathias was altering her brain chemistry so River could feel every sensation that came into her head. The ability to shove all her feelings into a dark corner was forever denied her. That, and her nascent psychic abilities, had presented Simon with a distressed, manic-depressive, paranoid, confused River who was considerably altered from the bratty genius he'd grown up with.

Now, though, she was back. Her wet eyes were clear for the first time since he liberated her eight months ago.

"I'm all right," she said again.

And Simon believed it.

Mal walked back in then, Inara on his arm. He only said two words: "Let's go."

Wash pulled the recording cylinder out of the console, and they all left the ship, the airstrip, the city, the planet as fast as they could.

SERENITY

Malcolm Reynolds stood in the dining hall of *Serenity,* his faith shattered.

He had thought that to have taken place eight years before, in the valley for which he gave this boat her name. Prior to that five-week battle and its two-week aftermath, he had been a God-lovin', God-fearin' man. But then Zoë spoke three fateful words: "They're not coming." The victory of the Alliance over the Independents showed Mal that, if there was a God, he was a right bastard, and Mal wanted no truck with Him, nor them that believed in Him.

But, though he'd not have cottoned to it till now, Mal still had some faith. True enough, he thought that the 'verse would as soon spit in your soup, but at least it gave you soup, he knew that much.

Until today. Today, when he watched so many good people get killed, when Shepherd Book died in his arms. That surely was a heinousness. But what made the knife twist a ways was that it was all to cover up a heinousness that made today, that made Serenity Valley, that made the whole war and all the misery that had come since, seem like a gorram birthday party.

Mal looked down at the dining table, where the cylinder lay. His faith was shattered, truly, but Shepherd Book's dying words to Mal were for him to believe in something, and right now Mal believed in this: The eight people in this room would not be the only ones to see what was on that cylinder.

Then he looked out at his crew. "This report is maybe twelve years old. Parliament buried it, and it stayed buried till River dug it up. This is what they feared she knew. And they were right to fear, 'cause there's a universe of folk that are gonna know it too. They're gonna *see* it. Somebody has to speak for these people."

He looked out at each of them. Jayne, looking more spooked than Mal had ever seen him. Wash, looking just as spooked, gripping Zoë's hand as tight as Mal had held Inara on Miranda. Zoë, cold fury on her face, making Mal truly fear for whoever was foolish enough to get in her way. Inara, as beauteous as ever, her own faith as shattered as Mal's. Kaylee, looking terribly sad, like a little one who found out that Santa ain't real, only about ten times worse; Mal knew that she felt for every single one of those poor dead folk, and Mal loved her for it. Simon, a fury of his own that Mal suspected could be as nasty in its own way as Zoë's, both for what the Alliance did to his sister, and what they did to them on Miranda.

And River, who actually looked sane for the first time since Mal laid eyes on her. That was probably scarier than Jayne, Zoë, and Simon put together.

"You all got on this boat for different reasons, but

you all come to the same place. So now I'm asking more of you than I have before. Maybe all. 'Cause as sure as I know anything, I know this: They will try again. Maybe on another world, maybe on this very ground, swept clean. A year from now, ten, they'll swing back to the belief that they can make people— better. And I do *not* hold to that. So no more running. I aim to misbehave."

Jayne stood up and grabbed a mug off the table. "Shepherd Book used to tell me: If you can't do something smart, do something right." He then took a big swig from the mug, then slid the mug down to Simon, who caught it. It was probably as much of a peace offering as Jayne would offer the doctor.

That wasn't nearly as telling to Mal as the fact that Jayne actually spoke for the entire crew. *These do be desperate times if that's the state of affairs.*

"Do we have a plan?" Simon asked.

"Mr. Universe. We haven't the equipment to broad-wave this code, but he can put it on every screen for thirty worlds. He's pretty damn close, too." As Mal spoke, Simon drank from Jayne's mug, then stopped quickly and looked suspiciously at it.

River spoke. "Based on our orbital trajectories, he reached optimum proximity just before our sunset. If we make a direct run within the hour, we're only three hundred sixty-seven thousand four hundred forty-two miles out. At full burn, we'd reach him inside of four hours."

Everyone stared at River a spell, as that was the most normal speech she'd ever given—if knowing the mileage 'twixt Miranda and Mr. Universe's little co-opted moon could be properly filed under "normal."

At that moment, Mal realized his faith *wasn't* shattered, not entirely. He had faith in one other thing: his crew. Wash and Zoë and Kaylee, of course, who'd been with him practically from the git-go; Jayne, for all his bluster and betrayal; Inara, for all she'd been just a renter, and for all she'd departed; and Simon and River, for all he tried to rid himself of them.

And Shepherd Book, may he rest in the peace I doubt I'll ever find.

Then Wash said, "Still got the Reavers, and probably the Alliance between us and him."

Zoë added, "It's a fair bet the Alliance knows about Mr. Universe. They're gonna see this coming."

"No." Mal's jaw tightened. "They're not gonna see *this* coming."

Then he went down to the cargo deck to suit up.

MR. UNIVERSE'S MOON

The operative watched as the person who called himself Mr. Universe spoke with Malcolm Reynolds.

"It's no problem," the man, who managed to be completely idle yet horrifically hyperactive simultaneously, was saying. "Bring it on bring it on bring it on! From here to the eyes and ears of the 'verse, that's my motto—or it would be if I start having a motto."

"We won't be long," Reynolds said with a curt nod.

"You're gonna get caught in the ion cloud, it'll play merry hob with your radar, but pretty pretty lights and a few miles after you'll be right in my orbit."

Reynolds looked impatient; he likely knew about the ion cloud already. *"You'll let us know if anyone else comes at you?"*

"You'll be the first."

A lie, of course. This Mr. Universe person was the most difficult of *Serenity*'s allies to track down. The Rample twins knew him only by his sobriquet. Like the operative, Mr. Universe had no real name that could be found. In addition, he seemed to have access to every wave that went throughout the system, whether it was communication, information, or entertainment.

That was a power that could not be afforded to anyone not working for the Alliance.

The operative removed the sword from his briefcase even as Mr. Universe turned his chair around toward him. "There. Toss me my thirty coin, but I got a newswave for you, friend—"

Whatever information this man wished to impart was lost as the operative ran him through. Mr. Universe seemed surprised, as if he could have all this information at his disposal, yet be wholly unaware of the usual fate of traitors.

Then Mr. Universe looked at the operative with confusion—and sadness. His face seemed to ask why he was doing what he was doing.

And the operative, just for a moment, felt pity.

Disgusted by this show of emotion, he pulled the sword out, and started to clean it. As he did so, he turned to Carmelito, who stood with several other soldiers. "Call in every ship in the quadrant. We'll meet them in the air." To the soldiers he said simply, "Destroy it all."

He followed Carmelito out the door, and they entered the shuttle that had docked at what once was a communications complex. Silently, the pilot steered it back as Carmelito passed the operative's orders on.

Within the hour, fifty-two ships were waiting outside the ion cloud through which *Serenity*'s course would take it. With their radar so mussed, they wouldn't see the operative's armada until it was far too late.

Cowardly, perhaps, but it got the job done. Though the operative often wished it were otherwise, the mission was paramount. He didn't have to do it right, he just had to do it.

Finally, after an interminable wait, the helmsman cried out, "I'm reading activity in the cloud!"

At last. Soon this would finally be over. This mission had gone on far longer than anyone could have predicted. Captain Reynolds was a more difficult foe than even the operative had imagined. *It's amazing the depths that hatred will drive a man to.*

"Lock and fire on my command." He sighed. "You should have let me see her. We should have done this as men, not with fire. . . ."

The cloud of ionized particles started to swirl with displacement, and then *Serenity* emerged. Or rather, a ship that was vaguely shaped like *Serenity.* It had been damaged, modified—been given a rather large cannon. Peering at the helmsman's console, he saw that the radiation readings were all wrong.

Then the operative smiled, realizing what Reynolds had done. He had made his ship over into the image of the Reavers. The operative had destroyed all the places *Serenity* could go to, but that just forced Reynolds to get creative. So he made over his ship and hid in Reaver territory.

By now, Reynolds had to see his armada. Even with that cannon on his backside, his cargo carrier was no match for any one of the ships under the operative's command, much less fifty-two of them. Opening a channel to the weapons room, he said, "Vessel in range, lock on." He shook his head. "Bastard's not even changing course."

Oddly, the ion cloud hadn't stopped swirling. In fact, it was moving at a great rate, as if several more—

No.

Fifty more ships came through the cloud. All of them in the same condition as *Serenity*—but they came by their radiation leakage, haphazard design, and extra paint jobs somewhat more honestly.

Reavers.

"That's not good," he said. Reynolds must have fired on the Reavers as he departed their space, getting them to follow. He *knew* it was a trap, knew that if the operative could find out about Haven, he could find out about the nameless corpse who'd stolen this moon.

So he set a trap of his own.

The helmsman, who no doubt thought the Reavers to be nothing more than a campfire tale, looked distinctly frightened. "Sir?" he asked in a voice that was more a high-pitched whine. Around him, all the other officers went pale with shock and fear. The Reavers were not wholly mindless—they designed their ships for the express purpose of inducing fear, and right now it was working too damn well.

"Target the Reavers!" He slammed the intercom to weapons. "Target the Reavers! Target everyone! Somebody *fire!*"

Eventually, somebody down in weapons had the wherewithal to fire, but by then *Serenity* was too close for them to get a good lock—especially once it dove to port.

The Reavers, however, were very much in range and several shots hit their ships.

It didn't slow them down.

Moments later, the battle was joined. Alliance ships fired at the Reavers. Reavers went on *kamikaze* runs straight at the Alliance ships.

And *Serenity* was heading right for the moon. *Dammit!*

You could have just handed her over, Reynolds. You could have made this simple. Instead, you have forced me to destroy so many people—and now you're providing some destruction of your own. This cannot possibly end in anything but more death. And you could have stopped it.

Reports of massive hull breaches sounded all around him. The computer soon informed him in both English and Chinese that life support was failing and that the reactor core in the engine was overloading.

Grabbing a sidearm off a soldier who died when a piece of the ceiling caved his skull in, the operative ran toward the darts, the one-person escape pods located in the lower decks of the ship. When he arrived, Carmelito—covered in blood that may or may not have been his own—was struggling to get into one of the crafts. The operative aided him and sent his dart into the black. Then he climbed into the one next to it.

It was the work of a moment to set the dart's course: the moon. It was Reynolds's destination, after all, and it was the operative's job to stop him.

The operative's stomach lurched as the dart flew down and out of the ship toward the moon. He looked out through the window at his command, which was breached in several dozen places, the engine burning with a fire that the vacuum consumed as fast as the engine created it.

A Reaver ship was heading straight for it. The operative winced as the Reaver vessel rammed his former command ship, destroying it. Carmelito's dart was caught in the backwash and also destroyed. The operative's own dart was tossed end over end, but was still intact as it made its way toward the largest gravitational field in the area.

Soon, Captain Reynolds, we will, at last, end this monstrosity.

—

It had been simple enough to get the Reavers to follow *Serenity*. Mal had removed the space-suited corpse that was at the cannon's controls on the ship's roof, and replaced it with his very own self.

As they flew through Reaver space, one ship started pacing them. When they got to the edge of Reaver territory, Mal "woke up," turned the cannon on that ship, and blew it into a lot of smaller pieces—though some of them were still big enough to go flying into a couple other Reaver ships, which also blew into bits. Mal then turned and fired the cannon a few more times for good measure.

True to plan, this made the other Reavers a mite ornery. At Mal's signal, Wash went to full burn, and they was off to the races.

A race that came to a satisfactory conclusion when *Serenity* flew out of the ion cloud into the expected

Alliance armada, four dozen Reaver ships flying up their posteriors with a serious mad-on.

Mal's only regret was that he didn't see the look on that glasses-wearing rutter's face when he saw the Reavers.

Was no easy thing, climbing to the airlock and reentering the ship while they were at full burn, but Mal managed it without being bucked off into the black. He pulled off his suit and went to the bridge, joining Zoë in watching Wash do what he did best.

Mal knew the plan worked when they'd been out of the ion cloud for a good ten seconds before any Alliance ship commenced to firing. By that time, they were in too close for them to get any kind of decent lock.

Wash listed to port and did a vertical three-sixty. Not that there was any up or down in space, but relative to the fleet, they were ass-end-up. Like threading a needle, Wash moved between the Alliance ships, most of which were too busy soiling their boxers or getting shot up by the Reavers to pay *Serenity* much mind.

Almost feeling the urge to smile, Mal said, "We're too close for them to arm."

Zoë was wearing her I-have-a-bad-feeling-about-this look. "This is gonna be very tight."

Jayne came onto the bridge, looked up through the window at the tops of Alliance ships. "Hey, look, we're upside down."

Mal rolled his eyes.

Meanwhile, Wash was in the Zen-like trance he

tended to when he had a particular rough bit of flying to do. "I am a leaf on the wind, watch how I soar."

Mal gave Zoë a look, but she just shrugged. After all, she only married him, that didn't obligate her to explain him.

Long as he gets us to Mr. Universe and his toys, he can be a boil on my foot for all I care.

They almost made it through when a barreling piece of debris flew right in their path. Wash yanked *Serenity* out of the way, but it put them back into the fray instead of moving safely away from it like Mal wanted.

He looked out at the chaos. As good as the Alliance was at violence, they were as babes in the woods compared to the Reavers. The Alliance had tactics and strategies that were guided by at least some token human concerns; the Reavers just had a vicious, unrelenting, uncaring brutality that knew nothing but itself.

"Chickens come home to roost," Mal muttered as *Serenity* came about and headed for the moon.

The ship jolted. "The hell—?" In order to duck a very big chunk of one Alliance ship, Wash had been forced to fly right into a smaller one.

All pretense of Zen-like trances out the window, Wash screamed, "It's okay! I am a leaf on the wind!"

"What does that *mean?*" Mal asked angrily.

Wash didn't answer, instead struggling with the controls. Mal couldn't help but notice that Wash's arm movements didn't correspond with the way *Serenity* was bucking and weaving like they was supposed to.

"We're fried!" Wash said, confirming what Mal saw. "I got no control!"

Mal ran to the console, trying and failing to get power back to the helm. He grabbed the intercom. "Kaylee, what the hell's goin' on down there? Wash can't fly, he ain't got controls!" There was no response. "Kaylee!"

"This is Simon," the doctor said over the line. *"Kaylee's been electrocuted—she'll be fine, it was just a minor shock, but the engine room's on fire. I had to seal it off."*

Letting out a particularly long and nasty curse in Chinese—one he'd been told wished either a flesh-eating disease or an uncontrolled bowel movement on one's enemy, depending on the inflection—Mal tried to get the backups online and also tried not to panic. "Where's the backup? Where's the backup?"

At the first of those, he succeeded—

"Backup reads at twenty percent," Zoë said.

—up to a point. Still, it was twenty percent more than they had with the primaries.

Zoë gave her husband her be-honest-with-me-sweetie look. "Can you get us down?"

"I'm gonna have to glide her in."

"Will that work?"

Wash let out a breath. "Long as that landing strip is made of fluffy pillows . . ."

Running that curse on repeat through his head, Mal grabbed the intercom again. "Everybody to the upper decks! Strap yourselves to something!"

The twenty percent was basically enough for Wash

to get *Serenity* pointed at the moon. That was important, since without that, they'd shoot past the moon and keep going till they ran out of power. Then they'd *still* keep going, thanks to inertia, until they hit something or died, the latter being the more likely of the two.

But it also meant that using the thrusters for braking was pretty much a forlorn hope. Wash put the landing gear down and headed straight for the landing strip outside the communications complex Mr. Universe had taken over.

Mal and Zoë strapped themselves into two of the chairs on the bridge. Mal prayed to Shepherd Book's God, Inara's Buddha, the great and powerful Zeus, and whatever other deity cared to stick his all-powerful nose in and let them survive this damn landing.

For a brief moment, Mal thought they were going to survive.

Then they actually hit the airstrip.

Mal took the screeching and tearing sound that ended all abrupt-like to be the landing gear being ripped to pieces. He felt himself being pulled to the side, the restraints biting into his ribcage, as Wash used the dregs of their twenty percent to turn the ship about, so she fishtailed on the strip, doing a full one-eighty, causing them to back into the hangar at the end of the strip.

More screeching metal, shorter this time, and Mal then saw the port thruster go flying into the air. *That's gonna make taking off entertaining,* Mal thought.

Still, that was the least of their troubles. The rear of the ship crashed into the back wall of the hangar.

Finally, *Serenity* came to a stop, having apparently crashed into enough things to promote deceleration.

The harness had kept Mal from flying about the bridge, but his entire body was sore from being shoved against it. He unbuckled it and stood up, trying very hard to remember that old saying about how any landing you can walk away from is a good one.

Wash turned to Zoë and Mal and grinned. "I am a leaf on the wind. Watch—"

Then the harpoon that was as thick as a tree crashed through the window and impaled Wash to the chair.

"Wash!"

Mal had known Zoë a fair amount of time. He didn't never hear such pain in her voice as he did right then, not even during the worst of Serenity Valley.

She ran to Wash, crying, "Wash, baby, baby, no, come on, you gotta move, you gotta move, baby, please—"

Looking up, Mal saw at least two Reaver ships, one of which was at the other end of the harpoon that just killed Wash. It was firing another one.

Grabbing Zoë, he ripped her away from her husband's body and out of the bridge before the second one also came crashing through, right at the spot where she'd been standing.

She tried to pull away, to run back inside, but Mal kept his grip on her. "Later, Zoë, later—he's *already dead!*"

Zoë stopped struggling, but the look on her face was one Mal had never seen there. In a choked voice, she said, "Wash . . ."

"I know, Zoë, I know." He had no idea how the *hell* they were going to leave this rock with only one thruster and without Wash's magic powers to get them off the ground. But that was a quandary that could sit awhile till the other business was took care of. "I need you focused, Zoë."

For one more second, Zoë Washburne, mourning wife, looked back at him. Then her face hardened, and she was Corporal Zoë Alleyne of the 57th again. "Let's go."

Mal nodded, and they ran down to the cargo deck. Everyone was armed and ready to storm the complex. River, Simon, and Kaylee looked uncomfortable with their guns, but Inara looked right natural with a bow and arrow in hand. Kaylee looked a mite frazzled from that electrocution Simon mentioned, but she looked ready to do what was needed. "Jayne, take point."

Jayne nodded, and moved to the airlock.

River looked at Zoë, then looked at Mal. A tear started to roll down her cheek.

She knows.

Mal said nothing, though, and neither did the girl.

From the airlock, Jayne cried, "Go!"

They all filed out of *Serenity.* Mal led the way toward the double-sized doorway that led to Mr. Universe's "black room," the entrance to his facility. When they got to the doorway, Mal hit a button, and blast doors opened from the sides, top, and bottom, widening the space something considerable.

"Come on, Jayne—rear guard," Mal said.

Zoë slowed. "Sir—this is a good hold point."

Shaking his head, Mal said, "We all stay together—"

"No."

Mal blinked. Zoë wasn't one for questioning his orders without good reason, and Mal wasn't too keen on her reasoning abilities right present.

"They have to come through here. They'll bottleneck, and we can thin 'em out. We get pushed back, there's the blast doors."

Kaylee put in, "I can rig 'em so they won't reopen once they close."

. That actually struck Mal as a better plan. "Then shut 'em and hide till—"

Zoë shook her head. "We need to draw them till it's done. *This* is the place. We'll buy you the time."

Much as Mal hated to admit it, it was a good plan. The last thing they needed was Reavers inside Mr. Universe's little sanctum.

He nodded.

Jayne looked at Simon, Inara, and River. "Move those crates back there for cover—and make sure they ain't filled with anything goes boom."

Kaylee blinked. "Wait, Wash—where's Wash?"

Before Mal could say anything, Zoë, the picture of dead calm—in all the senses of that particular phrase— said, "He ain't comin'."

Nobody moved. Tears welled in Kaylee's eyes.

Jayne got everyone's attention in his usual manner. "Move the gorram crates! Come on!"

Then Mal heard the screams. Not the agonized wailing of Reavers' victims, but the war cries of the Reavers themselves.

He and Jayne ran to the door to see at least a dozen running down the airstrip right for them.

Looking at Jayne, Mal said, "Tell me you brought 'em this time."

Smiling, Jayne pulled out two grenades, tossed one to Mal, and they both armed them. Jayne threw his out into the oncoming Reaver rush; Mal just rolled his out a spell, then slammed the door shut.

The room shook from the two explosions. This time screams of pain were mixed in with the war cries.

Mal moved to Zoë, loading her sawed-off. "Zoë—are you here?"

She looked up at him with her I'm-ready-to-kill look. "Do the job, sir."

He looked Zoë right in the eye. "You *hold!*"

Then he looked at the others. "Hold till I'm back."

Unlike the last time he said those words, Mal didn't pause to pray to a God he no longer gave two figs for before performing his mission. *You wanted me to believe in something, Shepherd, and I think I just might have found it. May it bring us all peace and happiness—or at least a big poke in the Alliance's eye.*

He paused as he passed Inara. Said nothing. Had nothing to say. But he wanted to make sure the last thing he saw before he went into the valley of death was her.

— —

Jayne checked Vera—his biggest, favoritest gun—and then went over to Zoë, as he was unliking of her particular facial expression.

231

"Captain's right," he told her. "Can't be thinking on revenge if we're gonna get through this."

Zoë fixed him with as serious a look as she could. "You really think any of us are gonna get through this?"

Jayne looked at the rest of their defense force: a Companion with a bow and arrow, and a mechanic, a girl, and a doctor holding guns they looked about as comfortable holding as Jayne would attending a meeting of the Holy Pacifists' Club.

He looked back at Zoë. *"I might."*

Then River started going all crazy again, which surprised Jayne only 'cause it had been at least a couple hours since she gone crazy last, and he was starting to worry about when she might go back to crazy. She was grabbing her head and muttering, "I can't shut them up," a problem Jayne could appreciate.

Simon, naturally, tried to comfort her, being such a wuss and all. "It's okay."

"They're all made up of rage, I can't—"

A thud came from the door, meaning one of them Reavers just slammed against it. Or maybe more than one, it was hard to tell. Jayne cocked Vera. "She picked a sweet bung of a time to go helpless on us."

Zoë said, "Jayne and I take the first wave. Nobody shoots 'less they get past our fire."

Jayne nodded and moved up to stand alongside Zoë. It was a good plan. *No sense in the Wimpy Brigade wastin' ammo 'less they have to.*

The banging on the door went on. Jayne figured it was only a few minutes before the Reavers would come through.

Simon walked over to Kaylee, who was shaking so much Jayne feared she'd vibrate through the floor or something. She also hadn't loaded her damn gun yet. Wasn't an issue right present, but Jayne didn't want nobody being ripped into Reaver kibble 'cause a nervous mechanic couldn't load her gun with speed.

"Oh, I didn't plan on going out like this." Kaylee was, in Jayne's opinion, just plain dumb; nobody planned how they went out. She kept jawing: "I think we did right, but . . ."

The doc sighed. "I never planned—anything. I just wanted to keep River safe. Spent so much time on *Serenity* trying to find us a home, I never realized I already had. My one true regret in all this is never being with you."

Jayne thought he was gonna throw up right there on the floor.

"With me?" Kaylee wasn't so shaky no more. "You mean to say, as, sex?"

Simon grinned that grin that always made Jayne want to punch him. "I mean to say."

Kaylee slammed her ammo pack into the pistol with a lot more precision than Jayne had ever seen her use a gun before. "Hell with this, I'm gonna *live.*"

Another bang on the door. Jayne was smiling, though. *We get outta this, Doc, I'm gonna be praisin' you on your motivational speakin'.*

The banging was joined by screeching, which meant the Reavers were starting to pry the door open. Jayne held up Vera.

When one Reaver's head—leastaways, Jayne

assumed it was his head, it was hard to tell with all the piercings, scars, and war paint, but he was pretty sure he sighted himself a nose—popped through, Zoë shot it in the head. Then another one popped out, and Zoë shot it—

—while walking *toward* the door, instead of holding the line like the captain said. Hell, like *good sense* said.

"Zoë, gorrammit—"

She moved closer, like she was in some kinda trance, shooting and shooting. One went at her with a blade, which she deflected right easy.

Then the door burst open, and Zoë was stuck among them Reavers.

With Vera set on auto, Jayne plowed through the lot of them, even though they kept coming.

"Zoë! Get yer ass back in the line!"

At that, Zoë looked up, all confused-like—then one of the gorram Reavers sliced at her back with a blade.

Before Jayne could do anything, an arrow got the Reaver right in the neck.

Inara. Who'da thunk it?

That gave Jayne the opening to drag Zoë back to where the doc could look at her. He kept Vera on auto, which kept the Reavers back for a spell.

"Spine's intact," Simon was saying while he looked at her.

"Just gimme a bandage."

Jayne smiled as he tossed a couple grenades through the door, killing a lot more Reavers. *That woman got*

234

fight in her. Maybe, with Wash cold, she'll think about trying a real man on for size.

While Simon did his medical magic on Zoë, Jayne kept shooting, since the Reavers kept coming. He was down to his last grenade. When Vera finally ran out, he tossed her aside and whipped out another gun. This one wasn't as big, and he hadn't gotten around to naming her, but she could fire a shot or twelve. Some Reavers got close enough that Jayne had to get more physical with them.

And then he felt a bullet buzz by his head.

Since when do the gorram Reavers use guns? "Oh, now you're *likin'* guns, huh? Cheaters!" He shot a few more to punctuate his disapproval.

Another bullet whizzed by, this one getting him in the shoulder. Jayne didn't let it bother him none, he just kept shooting.

A few darts went by Jayne's ear. Some landed in Kaylee, and she screamed and fell to the floor. *Reavers is definitely crazy—who the hell brings darts to a gunfight?*

"Everybody fall back—*fall back!*"

That was Zoë, who looked like she'd gotten her sense back while she was shooting Reavers from the floor. Jayne didn't like running, but he liked getting et a lot less. He ran back, Inara dragging Kaylee, Simon dragging Zoë, who wasn't too mobile.

Once they got into the corridor, Inara hit the button and the room started to close up again. But it didn't go all the way.

Zoë looked at him. "Jayne, grenade."

"Very last one." Jayne activated it and tossed it into the more-enclosed space.

Problem was, them Reavers would be getting through the door, which was exactly what they didn't want.

"They're gonna get in," Zoë said.

Kaylee sounded like hell when she said, "Can close it—from—outside—"

Zoë tried to stand up, but couldn't. "No one's coming back from that. How much ammo do we have?"

Jayne shook his head. "We got three full cartridges and my swingin' cod. That's all."

Inara had run over to the elevator and had hit the button about sixty times. "Lift isn't moving."

Fixing Jayne with one of those looks of hers, Zoë said, "When they come, try to plug the hole with 'em."

As Jayne nodded, Kaylee started screaming again. "I'm—starting to lose some feeling—here—I think there's something in them darts they throwed at me."

Simon walked over to her. "Lie still. I'm gonna give you something to counteract the—" When he got up, he looked over at Zoë. "My bag."

Then Jayne heard gunfire. He ran to flatten himself against the wall.

The doc wasn't that quick—bullet tore through his belly.

River opened her mouth like she was gonna scream, but no noise came out, which Jayne considered a kindness. Simon collapsed to the floor, blood spreading out all over his fancy shirt.

Inara ran up and put some kinda cloth on his stomach. "Keep pressure here."

236

"My bag." He sounded as whacked up as Kaylee. "Need—adrenaline—and a shot of calaphar for Kaylee—I can't—River?"

The crazy girl was kneeling down next to her brother.

"River, I'm—sorry—"

"No. No."

"I hate to—leave—"

Jayne fired into the hole, trying to keep the Reavers from pouring in. *Startin' to lose feelin' in my shoulder. Zoë can't walk, Kaylee's down, and the guy who can fix us got himself a belly wound. I ain't filled with the milk'a human optimism. And now River's gone crazy again.*

But she didn't sound crazy when she said, "You won't. You take care of me, Simon. You've always taken care of me."

Then the lights went out. *That's all we gorram need.*

Emergency lights came on but a second later, and everything was all red.

River was standing up now. "My turn."

Moving as fast as she moved in the Maidenhead, River ran straight *into* the hole.

"River!" That was Simon, who objected to the notion of his sister jumping into a room full of Reavers.

The last thing Jayne saw was the girl being overrun.

— —

The previous time Mal was in Mr. Universe's sanctum, it was well lit, screens showing all manner of things that weren't supposed to be looked at. And it was loud, speakers letting him hear all manner of things not meant to be heard.

This time, the place was dark and quiet.

So was Mr. Universe. He was dead, draped half over his Love-Bot™. There was a blood trail leading from his chair to the one Lenore lived on. All his computers, his equipment, his receivers, everything that had made him incredibly useful to Mal and incredibly dangerous to the Alliance, was destroyed.

And Mal had a fair guess which glasses-wearing gent was responsible. *Another one to add to the list.*

"Mal."

Looking over at the Love-Bot™, Mal realized that the voice—which sounded more than a little like Mr. Universe—was coming from her, and her eyes were all lit up.

"Guy killed me, Mal. He killed me with a sword. How weird is that? I got—a short span here—they destroyed my equipment, but I have a backup unit. Bottom of the complex, right over the generator. Hard to get to. I know they missed it. They can't stop the signal, Mal. They can never stop the signal. Okay, this is painful. On many levels. I'm not—"

Then Lenore powered down, her eyes going dark.

Mal went for the generator. The accessway was a long staircase that took him down to a catwalk. Peering over the railing, he looked down—way way down—to see the massive generator that kept Mr. Universe's little free-signal world going, full of grinding parts and arcs of electricity and such like. Kaylee could probably identify every part, but for Mal it was just the big scary thing near the thing he was looking for.

Then, finally, he saw it, on the other side of the generator from where he was standing: a broadwave console. In order to close the distance 'twixt here and there, Mal would need to crawl over all manner of ladders, cables, chains, and other like nonsense strung over the ceiling. Should he lose his grip, a fall into generator hell awaited him.

"Hard to get to. That's a fact."

He climbed up onto the railing, trying to reach the ladder run on the ceiling so he could start progressing. Seeing as how one misstep would send him to an early grave, he was very careful in the action.

Then he felt a burning pain in his back, and he lost his balance. Miraculously, he fell on the catwalk side of the railing instead of the generator side.

He looked up through a pain-induced haze to see the operative, looking more than a little worse for wear, holding a laser pistol. "Shot me in the back." He smiled sweetly. "I haven't made you angry, have I?"

The operative just stared at him through those damn specs. "There's a lot of innocent people in the air being killed right now."

Now he decides to get righteous. "You have *no* idea how true that is." He got to his feet, facing the operative. "I know the secret. The truth that burned up River Tam's brain and set you after her. And the rest of the 'verse is gonna know it, too. 'Cause they need to."

"You really believe that?" The operative sounded pitying.

"I do."

"You willing to die for that belief?"

"I am."

Satisfied with that answer, the operative started to raise his laser.

Unsatisfied with dying in that manner, Mal whipped out his pistol and shot the laser right out of his hand. He got two more shots to the operative's still-armored chest before they both ran for cover behind some machines that served a purpose Mal could only guess and not care about.

Dropping out his ammo cartridge and putting in a fresh one, he muttered, "Of course, that ain't exactly Plan A. . . ."

The operative stuck his head out, and Mal shot at it until he ducked back again.

As much fun as duck huntin' is, I got bigger fish to fry. Holstering his gun, he ran for the railing, and jumped up to one of the rungs. He went hand over hand across the rungs, trying to get to the broadwave before the operative cottoned to the fact that Mal wasn't shooting at him no more.

That last part of the plan didn't work so good. The operative ran over to his laser, looked at it, then didn't pick it up. Mal's guess was, his shot blew it out. *Alliance hardware ain't all it's cracked up to be.*

The operative then did the same thing Mal did, except he leapt and grabbed one of the chains bunched up at the ceiling. It snapped, but the operative still swung across to grab another chain.

Even as Mal tried to get to the broadwave, the operative got a damn sight closer, and kicked Mal right in the back in the same spot where he was shot. Pain sliced through his entire chest, and his arms went briefly numb. Somehow, flailing about, Mal managed to grab another chain and hang on to it for dear.

Mal tried to kick the operative, but it was no use, he moved too fast. Though Mal was the faster draw, the operative was faster at just about everything else. Including swinging over to the wall to pull some kind of lever.

His stomach lurching, Mal found himself suddenly about ten feet lower as the chain loosened thanks to whatever the operative did, and he was swinging toward the wall under the railing.

Oh, this is very not good. He slammed into the wall with a bone-stinging thud.

The good news was, he was where he wanted to be, if a few feet downward. Forcing himself not to think about the pain in his back—and his front, his side, his top, his bottom, and his entire middle—Mal climbed up the chain, the cold metal digging into his fingers, eyes on the broadwave at the top of the chain.

Just as he clambered up to the top and over the railing, he saw the operative. Gone was the calm demeanor with which he had massacred the good folks of Haven. Now he was unkempt, his pretty uniform all nice and mussed, and he was right pissed off.

Well, good, Mal thought as he unholstered his gun. *Guess fifty Reaver ships didn't sit well with his sin-free 'verse.*

The operative tackled Mal, knocking him to the

floor and forcing him to lose his grip on the gun. It went sliding across the floor, under the railing, and over the edge into the abyss.

Not so good. Mal managed to get in a hammer blow or two, which got him off. *That proves he's losin' it. No chance that woulda worked back at Inara's place. The man's off his feed something fierce.*

Feeling at something less than his best himself, Mal stumbled into a tool chest, which clattered to the floor with loud clanks as computer parts and tools hit the floor.

Reaching behind his back, the operative unsheathed that damn sword of his. *It's Persephone all over again.* There, he'd been thrown in the deep end of a duel thanks to his own big mouth, and Atherton Wing right near killed him when they faced off. Then, Mal had a like weapon to Wing.

Now, he had a screwdriver.

Also a toolbox, which he threw at the operative, then rushed him, trying to stab him in the neck with the screwdriver.

The operative blocked that, and got the sword's point right at Mal's stomach.

Tzao-gao!

Sword metal, Mal learned as the blade sliced into his stomach and all the way through to the other side, was very cold and coarse. He'd thought it would be smoother for some reason.

And painful—it was that a whole lot.

For the first time since Mal shot at him, the operative spoke. "You know what your sin is, Malcolm?"

Smiling, Mal said, "Aw, hell, I'm a fan of all seven." Then he head-butted the operative, following it up with a punch sufficiently hard to make the operative lose his grip on the sword in Mal's gut. The operative tried a spin-kick, but Mal managed to block it with the screwdriver, which he used to impale the operative's boot. Mal pulled the screwdriver in toward him and socked the operative on the jaw. It hurt Mal's knuckles to do that, but when you had a big old sword in your gullet, pain became a mite relative.

Mal looked down on the operative, who had fallen to the floor thanks to Mal's punch. Grimacing, Mal gripped the hilt of the sword and slowly pulled it out. The pain when it went in was as nothing compared to the white-hot agony that burned through his entire chest when he pulled it out.

He held up the sword over the operative's face. "But right now, I'm gonna have to go with wrath."

To Mal's irritation, his attempt to stab the man in the face was stymied by the operative's rolling away. Pain shot through his leg as the operative kicked Mal, forcing him to stumble. Then the operative stood up and punched Mal in the belly wound, which set his entire stomach on fire, and made the rest of his body ice cold.

—

Jayne knelt near Zoë. They hadn't heard a gorram thing from the Reavers since the crazy girl went and dove into them. Since it wouldn't take them but a

243

minute to turn her into crazy cutlets, Jayne's way of thinking was that it was the Maidenhead River, not the regular River, since all the regular River was like to do was confuse them to death.

Still, Jayne had his weapon ready. He'd reloaded as much as he could; so had Zoë. Inara was keeping an eye on Simon, trying to keep the doc from bleeding *all* over the floor, and Kaylee was lying still since Inara gave her that shot of whatever-it-was that the doc told her to give before he commenced to passing out.

Jayne was getting antsy, as not having nothing to shoot was like to do to him. Jayne looked at Zoë. Even all injured-like, she was as intimidating as anybody Jayne ever knew—and he knew some right intimidating folk, starting with his own self. "You think he got through? Think Mal got the word out?"

Zoë didn't have no doubts. "He got through. I know he got through."

Frankly, Jayne figured Mal was dead and gone by now, same as the doc was like to be when that belly wound got through with him, same as the crazy girl would be once the Reavers finished lunchtime.

Same as they all would be.

Guess we got us our very own Serenity Valley right here on this go-se *rock.*

\-\-

Through careful training and conditioning, the operative did not feel anger or rage or inappropriate emotions of any kind when he was on a mission—generally.

Right now, however, he was taking great pleasure in kicking the shit out of Malcolm Reynolds.

The Companion had been correct—Reynolds *was* capable of reversing over a decade of the finest training in the Alliance and pissing the operative off. And the fact that he had done so just angered him all the more. So it was with more than precision, more than the knowledge of the damage he would cause, that led him to kick Reynolds in the face.

It was anger.

After a moment, however, he got himself under control. He was better than this, made of worthier stuff than a common thug like Reynolds.

No, not a thug. Perhaps I was also wrong about him being a plucky hero. Either way, though, this must end.

He picked Reynolds up and got his battered, bloody self into a standing position. "I'm sorry." And he meant it. It was only a pity that Reynolds's passionate hatred for the Alliance was so much a part of what made him so formidable, because he would have made *such* a talented operative.

Then, as he had with Philbert Mathias and Derrial Book, he whirled Reynolds around and slammed his fingers into a nerve cluster in the back that would leave the captain paralyzed.

As Reynolds stood rigid, the operative walked over to his fallen sword. "You should know there's no shame in this. You've done remarkable things. But you're fighting a war you've already lost."

He thrust with the sword—

—and Reynolds, impossibly, ducked out of the way!

The operative stood in mute shock at this patent impossibility. That gave Reynolds all the opportunity he needed to grab the operative's sword arm, yank it and him forward, and then elbow him in the throat.

Gasping, choking, wheezing, the operative dropped his sword and stumbled back, unable to speak.

Reynolds grinned raggedly. "Well, I'm known for that." Then the captain grabbed the operative into a wrestling hold and cracked his arms.

It was a relatively simple maneuver, and it all but won the fight for one simple reason: The operative hadn't felt pain of this kind in *years*. Not since the earliest days of his training. He had forgotten how debilitating pain could be. He was *so* good, so skilled, so successful that no opponent had ever even seriously challenged him, much less hurt him.

Reynolds dropped him to the floor, the impact against the cold floor simply adding to the agony coursing through the operative's arms. Then the captain picked up the sword. "Piece'a shrapnel tore up that nerve cluster my first tour. Had it moved."

The operative cursed himself for once again failing to put disparate pieces of information into a coherent whole. At the training house, he hadn't connected the Companion's training with an ability to fight him; now, he did it again. He'd read Reynolds's medical records from the war, had seen the military surgeon's report on the operation that moved that cluster, but never thought to apply it to a hand-to-hand strategy. To be fair, he never expected to *require* a hand-to-hand strategy with Reynolds, either.

"Sorry 'bout the throat." Reynolds's apology sounded considerably less sincere than the operative's had been. "Expect you'd wanna say your famous last words now. Just one trouble."

He reached over the railing, pulled the back of the operative's jacket through and sliced the sword into the fabric—not through the operative's heart, as expected. Now he was pinned to the railing, unable to move, especially with his arms as damaged as they were.

"I ain't gonna kill you. Hell, I'm gonna grant you your greatest wish." He walked over to the broadwave console, removed a cylinder from his pocket, and put it in the player, turning it slightly to the right to lock it in. Then he hit the SEND ALL button. "I'm gonna show you a world without sin."

The screen on top of the broadwave lit up with images from an official Alliance report. The operative saw a city in ruins, and the voice of a woman saying, *"These are some of the first sites we scouted on Miranda. There is no one living on this planet. There is no one—except for a small few."* The image switched a few more times, showing the same death and destruction, then went to the person speaking, who wore an Alliance uniform, and looked quite shaken. *"These are just a few of the images we've recorded, and you can see it isn't—it isn't what we thought. There's been no war here, and no terraforming event. The environment*

247

is stable. It's the Pax—the G-32 paxilon hydrochlorate that we added to the air processors. It's—" The woman started to cry. *"—well, it works. It was supposed to calm the population, weed out aggression. Make a peaceful— It worked. The people have stopped fighting."*

Sometime during this, Reynolds had found the control to extend a ramp from the broadwave back to the catwalk. The operative barely noticed him leave, fascinated as he was by what he saw on Miranda.

--

Clutching his bleeding belly in what he figured to be a pretty damn futile attempt to keep the sword wound closed, Mal stumbled out of the elevator. Kaylee was down for the count, but with no obvious injuries. Simon was bleeding from a belly wound of his own; Inara's success in keeping him from bleeding was only slightly better than Mal's was for his own. Zoë was on her back and in obvious pain. Jayne had a shoulder wound, though you wouldn't know it to look at his face. Inara was the only one unhurt.

And River was nowhere to be seen.

Neither were the Reavers.

Zoë looked at Mal. "Sir?"

"It's done." Everyone seemed to exhale at that. "Report."

Before Zoë could say anything, the blast doors started to open. Jayne raised his weapon, as did Zoë. Inara reached for her bow. Mal tried to pull his gun, winced in agony at that particular arm movement, then declined to continue.

The door opened to reveal a blood-spattered, but not noticeably wounded, River Tam, holding a Reaver blade in each hand. She was standing in a very big sea of Reaver corpses.

Several curses went through Mal's head, all of them woefully inadequate.

Then Mal noted the grappling hooks in the wall, and was thinking this whole thing might not be as over as he thought a second past.

Sure enough, the walls were ripped away with a crack that near deafened Mal, to reveal a whole passel of Alliance soldiers. River may've done a job with them Reavers, but she also cleared the path for these more coherent folk.

"Drop your weapons! Drop 'em now!"

Jayne, Zoë, and Inara did so, Jayne with some reluctance.

"Do we engage? Do we engage?"

The first soldier spoke into a com unit. "Targets are acquired! Do we have a kill order? *Do we have a kill order?*"

Mal assumed they were talking to his friend with the glasses, who was upstairs getting a lesson in Alliance politics.

"Stand down," the operative finally said. *"We're finished."*

Each of the three graves had a jar atop it that contained a snap. The first showed Mr. Universe and his Love-Bot™, the former wrapping his arms around the latter in a warm embrace, Lenore being her usual aloof self. The name MISTER UNIVERSE was carved into the gravestone.

The second showed a wise-looking man with a silver goatee and wild hair tied into neat cornrows. He was smiling as if he knew the punch line to a joke that the 'verse wasn't quite ready to share with everyone else yet. The name on his stone read SHEPHERD DERRIAL BOOK.

The third was of a man wearing both a hideously loud shirt and a huge grin, using a set of toy dinosaurs in a play whose details were unimportant. HOBAN WASHBURNE. Or, simply, "Wash," as any man in his right mind would prefer to be known if the alternative was "Hoban."

A fourth stone sat next to them, but it housed, not a grave, but a rocket with various slips of paper attached to it. River attached a final slip to it and backed away to stand beside her brother. Simon put one hand on

River's shoulder, the other hand clasped tightly in Kaylee's. A crutch was wedged in the armpit of the hand that held River.

Next to them was Jayne, then Mal, holding Inara in much the same way Simon held River.

They all moved aside for Zoë, who wore a white funeral gown, holding a burning taper.

Silently, she walked up to her husband's grave. Then she went to the fourth stone and lit the rocket.

It shot into the dark sky of Haven, of the place they had all called refuge at least once, now a dead world, sacrificed to save the Alliance a bit of embarrassment.

Once the rocket hit its apogee, it exploded into a spectacular display of fireworks.

The crew of *Serenity* stood together, watched, and mourned.

PERSEPHONE

It was raining on the day *Serenity* was ready to take off.

Mal stood near the cargo ramp, sheltered from the downpour by *Serenity*'s nose, getting ready to board her and take her into the sky for the first time since they limped to the repair station at Eavesdown Docks. Fitting, really, since this was where they'd picked up Simon, River, and Book, that this was where they'd get fixed. It wasn't the best repair stop in the 'verse, but it was closest, and there was only so far they'd get with only one thruster.

'Specially without Wash to fly her.

It had taken some time, but they removed the cannon, fixed the self-inflicted damage, as well as that done by the Reavers and the Alliance, and replaced both the thruster and the landing gear. They might have got it done a day or two sooner, but Kaylee and Simon kept letting themselves get all distracted-like to a degree that Mal suspected his mechanic not to be needing her batteries for some time.

Mal winced. *Now why did I let my mind stray in that direction? Gonna need to brillo that one out of my brainpan. . . .*

Everyone pitched in. Zoë replaced the window that had been shattered by the harpoon that killed Wash. Jayne and Mal removed the cannon. Simon and River helped Kaylee with the technical stuff, though that was slowed by the random smooching. And Inara had repainted the name SERENITY in both English and Chinese on the ship's nose with her usual elegant hand.

Now, though, it was time to get back to the sky. Time to get back to flying.

There was, naturally, one bit of unfinished. Seemed there always was. Mal wasn't sure how long the operative had been standing near—easy to sneak in the rain, especially for them that was trained to it—but he did hear him walk closer. "If you're here to tell me we ain't finished—then we will be real quick."

The operative joined Mal by the ramp. "Do you know what an uproar you've caused? Protests, riots, cries for a recall of the entire parliament."

"We've seen the broadwaves."

"You must be pleased."

Mal winced as he turned toward the operative, the pain in his stomach managing to bully its way past the painkillers Simon had been giving him. The wound was just the latest in a series—Mal was fair sure he had more scars than skin nowadays—but it was still a mite tender.

"'Verse wakes up a spell. Won't be long 'fore she rolls right over and falls back asleep. T'ain't my worry."

"I can't guarantee they won't come after you—the

253

parliament. They have a hundred men like me and they are *not* forgiving."

That prompted a smirk from Mal. "That don't bode especially well for *you*—giving the order to let us go, patching up our hurt. . . ."

Shrugging, the operative said, "I told them the Tams were no longer a threat—damage done. They might listen, but—I think they know I'm no longer their man."

If the operative was angling for sympathy, he was barking up the wrong tree. Fact, he was in the wrong forest. "They take you down, I don't expect to grieve overmuch. Like to kill you myself, I see you again."

"You won't. There is—" He smiled grimly. "—nothing left to see."

Mal stared at this self-proclaimed monster, to whom he owed his life, and to whom he owed any number of deaths. All three of those grave markers on Haven, and hundreds besides, could be laid right at this man's feet. And yet, when he had every reason to give the kill order, he told his people to patch up Mal and his crew and let them go.

The second thing was what kept Mal from shooting him in the face for the first thing. For now, anyhow.

Mal walked up the cargo ramp, ready to leave this man very far behind. Meanwhile, the operative looked up at where Inara had repainted the boat's name. *"Serenity.* You lost everything in that battle. Everything you had, everything you were—how did you go on?"

I found something to believe in. But Mal wasn't

about to share intimates with this person. Turning around and pressing the button that would close the ramp and the inner door, Mal said, "You still standing there when the engine starts, you never will figure it out." The door shut. "What a *whiner.*"

Zoë was waiting for him inside. "Sir, we have a green light. Inspection's pos, and we're clear for upthrust."

"Think she'll hold together?"

Giving him her we're-fine-stop-worrying-so-damn-much look, Zoë said, "She's tore up plenty, but she'll fly true."

Mal looked at Zoë, who had been his right hand so long, he didn't think he knew how to function without her. *May it be a considerable spell of time 'fore I find out.* "Make sure everything's secure. Could be bumpy."

"Always is."

Ain't that the truth, Mal thought as he headed upstairs.

On the catwalk heading toward the bridge, he saw Inara. "We're taking her out. Should be about a day's ride to get you back to your girls."

"Right."

Mal moved past her, though something sounded a mite off in her tone. "You ready to get off this heap and back to a civilized life?"

"I, uh—"

That hesitation made Mal stop and look at her.

"I don't know."

He couldn't help but smirk at that. "Good answer."

Mal still wasn't rightly sure where he stood with

255

Inara, but he damn sure knew that this time he wasn't going to let her go without a fight.

He entered the bridge to find River in the copilot's seat. Mal moved to sit in Wash's old chair, taking a moment to adjust his dinosaurs. "You gonna ride shotgun, help me fly?" he asked the girl.

"That's the plan."

"Think you can work out how to get her in the—?"

Before Mal could finish asking, she answered by doing the entire start-up sequence without hesitating, including taking off.

"Okay," Mal said, trying not to sound as nonplussed as he truly felt, "clearly some aptitude for the— But it ain't all buttons and charts, little albatross. You know what the first rule of flying is?" He chuckled. "Well, I suppose you do, since you already know what I'm about to say."

"I do. But I like to hear you say it." River smiled. She had, Mal noticed, a good smile, like someone who took joy in everything around her. Way back when they first came on board, Simon said that the whole reason she went to that laughing academy in the first place was because she wanted to learn, and Mal was, for the first time, seeing that side of her.

He looked up at the window, rain spattering on it so fast it sounded like meat sizzling on a grill.

"Love. You can learn all the math in the 'verse, but you take a boat in the air you don't love, she'll shake you off just as sure as the turning of worlds. Love keeps her in the air when she oughtta fall down, tells you she's hurting 'fore she keens. Makes her a home."

Mal thought about Wash. He had a rep when Mal found him, and had offers from more ships than Mal could count. But he took the job on *Serenity,* even though lots of piloting work was a lot less hairy. And it wasn't because of Zoë—that happened slow-like over time—no, it was because Wash fell for this ship. Not the same way as Mal did, or Kaylee, or Inara, or River, but he did. That, as like as his skills, was why he always kept her flying. Mal's gaze strayed over to the dinosaurs. He'd considered putting them away, but no better tribute to Wash could be left on the boat than having his toys still watching over the bridge like always.

"Storm's getting worse."

At River's words, Mal looked back out the window. "We'll pass through it soon enough."

Then something ripped off the nose of the ship and flew up and away into the stratosphere at a great rate.

"What was that?"

> *And I had done an hellish thing,*
> *And it would work 'em woe:*
> *For all averred, I had killed the bird*
> *That made the breeze to blow.*
> *Ah wretch! said they, the bird to slay*
> *That made the breeze to blow!*
>
> —Samuel Taylor Coleridge,
> *The Rime of the Ancient Mariner*

ABOUT THE AUTHOR

This is **Keith R.A. DeCandido**'s second Joss Whedon novelization (following 1999's *Buffy the Vampire Slayer: The Xander Years* Volume 1, which novelized three *Buffy* episodes focusing on the character of Xander Harris), his second novelization of a movie featuring Adam Baldwin (following 1998's *Gargantua,* written as K. Robert Andreassi), and overall his fifth novelization (following the two above, *Resident Evil: Genesis, Resident Evil: Apocalypse,* and *Darkness Falls*). His fiction has taken him to various other media universes, including *Star Trek,* Marvel Comics, *Gene Roddenberry's Andromeda, Farscape, Doctor Who, Xena,* and more. His other recent and upcoming novels include *Dragon Precinct* (a high fantasy police procedural), *Star Trek: A Time for War, A Time for Peace* (a *USA Today* best-seller), *Enemy Territory* (the third book in the popular *Star Trek: I.K.S. Gorkon* series), *Ferenginar: Satisfaction Is Not Guaranteed* (part of *Worlds of Star Trek: Deep Space Nine* Volume 3), *Articles of the Federation* (a *Star Trek* version of *The West Wing,* showing a year in the life of the Federation president), *Spider-Man: Down These Mean*

Streets (Keith's fourth piece of prose fiction starring the web-swinger), and *Warcraft: Cycle of Hatred* (based on the popular game). He lives in New York City with his girlfriend and two insane cats with a wide array of books, CDs, videos, and DVDs (the latter including the complete set of *Firefly,* purchased the day of release). Find out all sorts of things you couldn't care less about regarding Keith at his official Web site at DeCandido.net.

**FROM THE MIND OF JOSS WHEDON
CREATOR OF *BUFFY THE VAMPIRE SLAYER* AND *ANGEL*
COMES HIS UNIQUE VISION OF THE FUTURE...**

This essential companion to the movie features:

- **A special Introduction by Joss Whedon**

- **An in-depth interview with him about the making of the film**

- **The full shooting script, including scenes cut from the final edit**

- **Fascinating production and background memos by Joss, including 'A Brief History of the Universe, circa 2507 A. D.'**

- **Scores of stunning movie stills, storyboards and pieces of production art**

Serenity
Joss Whedon
ISBN 1 84576 082 4
£16.99 $19.95
9" x 12" 280 x 215mm
Paperback Full color

YOU CAN'T STOP THE SIGNAL

Available from all good bookstores

TITAN BOOKS
www.titanbooks.com

TB2795

Not sure what to read next?

Visit Pocket Books online at
www.SimonSays.com

Reading suggestions for
you and your reading group

New release news

Author appearances

Online chats with your favorite writers

Special offers

And much, much more!